The Art of Cheating Episodes: S2E1

Cyber Pimpin'

EXTENDED AUTHOR'S CUT EDITION

HoLLyRod

COPYRIGHT

Cheater's Therapy
TAOC Prelude (Vol. 2)
Episode I

<u>November 2011</u>

"Ok then, Mister Henderson. You *are* persistent – I'll give you that much."

"Wait, hold on. What you mean by that???" I wondered, slightly annoyed about her sudden interruption.

"I think you know what I'm thinking."

I squinted my eyes, trying desperately to read my therapist's mind. But, as usual, Dr. Julie sat still and without expression – reading *me* carefully, waiting on *my* reaction. All I could do was shake my head at the brief silence, genuinely stumped.

"What? I know you ain't saying you don't agree with me?!?" I asked out of half-curiosity, but I was more focused on not losing track of my recent train of thoughts.

"Annnd…technically, with *that* question – wait, that was a question, right? Yeah, that was a question. With that question, you just did it yet *again*, my friend," her face beamed up with mischief. "Very consistent, indeed."

"Maaan…what are you talking about?!? What did I do?!?" I threw my hands up in confusion. "I thought we was talking about my *journey* – how I got in this drama."

"Yes, that's right," she agreed. "We're retracing your steps."

"Right! You asked me to think about everything that coulda led to this outcome, so that's all I'm doing! And now that I'm thinking about it, I'm just saying I can see the pattern! I been chasing that fantasy for a long time, Doc. Real talk."

Dr. Julie frantically shook her head at me, "But what you did just *now* is the more *relevant* pattern, Rodney."

"What did I *do*, though? You losing me again, DJ."

"Focus, Mister Henderson. Breathe."

I let out a deep breath, following her instructions almost out of reflex. I was used to this type of back and forth sparring after retaining **Dr. Julie Lott** as my head doctor for the last 4 years. We had great chemistry, and her style was perfect for me. She was tough and stern with a knack for forcing one to acknowledge some of the obvious flaws they stayed in denial about. I could tell that this was yet another one of those moments, but I wasn't able to put my finger on where exactly she wanted to take me this time.

"Thaaat's it. Take a deep breath…and let's…start over," she urged with encouragement.

"Start over?! From the beginning?" I gasped.

"Heavens, no! I only want you to back up just a little – before the **Club Ménages** days. And *this* time, try not to skip around and leave anything out."

"But I didn't *skip around,* Dr. Julie. I didn't leave anything out."

"Sure, you did," she pointed at me. "You've developed quite the habit of skipping around, leaving key details out. We've talked about this before, Rodney."

I rolled my eyes, "Ugh! But I didn't do it *this time* – like, for real, man."

"I call bs," Dr. Julie clicked her pen firmly, before switching gears. "How long have you been coming to these sessions now, Mister Henderson?"

"Four years, off and on," I shook my head. "Since right after Ronnie caught her case."

"Now I'd like to think that after *four years* – I know my patients better than you're wanting to admit in this moment."

"I'm not saying you don't – I don't mean it like that. I'm just saying I've been open today. I ain't leave nothing out."

"Do you remember what our sessions were like in the beginning? What made you first start coming to therapy? Besides getting approved off work, of course?" she smiled, trying to get me to let my guard down again.

I sighed once more, irritated at not being able to finish my rant without all of this overanalyzing, "I was having panic attacks and losing sleep."

"Because of your sister, right?"

"Yes. Her being flashed on the news and going on the run triggered me. My memories. Experiences from our childhood that we never addressed."

"The unresolved trauma; the toxic abuse the two of you endured. You reached a breaking point and..."

"And it was time to get help," I cut her off, my breathing pattern gradually slowing down. "The PTSD caught up with me and my body was shutting down."

"Bingo!" she clicked her pen again. "And do you remember the first piece of advice I gave you? Your first homework assignment?"

"Yeah. You told me that I have to '*acknowledge where I've **been** if I'm gonna ever see where I may be **going**'*. You said I gotta *reflect with objection*…and never give myself a *biased narrative*."

"Oh, so you *have* been paying attention to a little, old white lady, huh?" she smirked.

"But you said I did it again here *today*."

"Correct. You've been doing it ever since I've known you, Rodney. You go off on these rants and I sit here and jot and scribble in my notepad until you end up on another wild tangent. And like I said, these days I can see it coming from a mile away. So, I'll let you in on a secret. Whenever you're about to leave something out…or skip around…you usually do one of three things."

"Man, come on, man," I shook my head again before staring out the window to my far right.

"You'll either look out that window at that view of the gravel parking lot you love so much," she continued calmly as I pouted. "Or you'll drift off momentarily in mid-sentence, before rubbing your forehead with one thumb firmly – like *this*. When you start talking again, it's usually with a lower, more gathered tone – as if you've thought out your next words carefully and with strategic intent."

"Maaaan, stop playing, Dr. Julie."

"The first time you did this was when we were reflecting about what lured Ronnie to the street life. Do you remember? Can you recall what key detail you tried to avoid talking about then?"

"Nah, hold on…that was different!" I shot back in total disagreement.

"You talked to me about the neighborhood and the environment in the projects. You told me about the gangs and how strangely fascinated Ronnie was about the street life at the earliest of ages. And then your voice drifted off and you rubbed a nice dent in your forehead before continuing."

I kept shaking my head as my memory was jolted. I remembered that session like it was yesterday. Dr. Julie let me finish ranting that day until the timer clock started buzzing. But when our next session started, she called me out and told me to start over with the story, as if we hadn't talked about it the prior week. She told me that she knew I had left certain details out, but she never mentioned how she was so sure.

"And when you came back the next week, we were able to uncover a whole set of *other elements* you wanted to block out of your memory. Unbiased narratives – do you remember? Sometimes, the mind works extra hard to not revisit certain memories – so our ego doesn't go hungry."

"Yeah, I remember," I told her. "But you saying that I got a pattern of doing that…and I'm just not seeing it."

"You've done it many a time since then, Mister Henderson. Again, you have to remember I've been doing this a long time. And this isn't your first walk in the park with me, Rodney."

"Ok, but – *today?* I mean, I know I ain't rubbed my forehead at all…and I *just* looked out the window after you stopped me talking! I know I ain't left nothing out – not today, man! Like…come on!"

"Up until a few weeks ago…I hadn't seen you in quite some time – no?"

"Yeah…it's been a little over a year. Not since I moved back to Saint Louis."

"And why is that, Rodney? What made you start coming back *this time?* Why did you start making these trips up and down the highway…just for therapy? It wasn't Ronnie going back to prison. This time it was…*something else.*"

"Well, yeah – I told you. It's all this stuff I'm dealing with going back and forth with Sug."

"You mean **'Bonita'.**"

"Yeah," I sighed at her correcting me. "Bonita/Sug – same difference."

"You felt like this path you've been on with *Bonita* had you taking backwards steps. Something in your soul recognized that it was time to get help, much like that feeling in your gut when you first came to see me all those years ago."

"Ok, I'll buy that. I did. I felt like I was losing myself again and I wanted to break free. You were the only outlet I could think of."

"You know you're like a grandson to me, Rodney. And you will always have an open seat on my black couch. But the point I'm making is that *this time around*, what you needed healing with *wasn't* family or childhood related."

"Right. Not this time."

"Or *was it?*" she challenged. "Are we sure about that?"

"Uhmm. Yeah…I mean. I think there's a lot of layers to it, ya know what I'm saying? But this ain't about *childhood* shit this time, Dr. Julie. This is very much related to my *adult* life – chasing all of the fantasies. *That's* what got me here with Sug. Now I got habits I can't break."

"And what habits are those?" she asked in her best clueless voice.

"Man, come on, man," I rolled my eyes. "We been talking about this, man."

"Yes, and I want you to say it. Not for me. I want

you to acknowledge what *you* think this is about. Unbiased narratives, remember?"

"Yeah yeah…*unbiased narratives*. That's what I'm saying – I ain't leave nothing out this time, Dr. Julie!!"

"So, back up just a little for me. Before you met Bonita…before all of the *ménages* – as you like to call them."

"But that's what I was just talking about. When I met *George* and *Carol!*"

"No, forget about George and Carol for a minute. Forget about *Sashé* and how things seemed 'perfect' when you two finally found a playmate. This isn't about the ménages."

"What?!?!" I turned my lip up. "How come it's not? This is all about the fantasy I was chasing – if I was never chasing ménages…"

"Yes, but Rodney," she cut me off again. "You came to me with a much larger issue than just a sex-crazed addiction. Remember? The dark path?"

"Right – the pimping, the stripper parties, the money hustles. But all of that is the domino effect from going after fantasies! That's the *pattern.*"

"I beg to differ, Mister Henderson. There's something else, something deeper to it than that. In fact – dare I say – I don't think this latest hill you're climbing has anything to do with *sex* at all."

"Maaaaan," I started rubbing my forehead. "You

can't be serious right now."

"You don't pay me for my sense of humor, I'm sure."

"So, what is the deeper issue…if it's not fantasy or sex related? What is you saying I left out this time? The *cheating?*"

"If we dig deeper, I'm confident we'll find it's not about the cheating *or* the sex, Mister Henderson. But in order to do that, I need you to be honest with me. Be honest with *yourself*…because no one else will benefit from this more than you, Rodney."

"But I've been honest…like…that's what I'm saying! I been in here pouring my damn heart out about all dis shit! I left *KeLLy* because *Sashé* was willing to have *ménages* and KeLLy wasn't. Then, bringing other girls in the bedroom tore me and Shay apart. She was greedy, I was greedy. We tried to patch it up but I was bitter from her walking out. Sug came in the picture and by then I was knee-deep in the chase! I fell for Sug cuz she was on the same *wild sex* shit! How do you not see the pattern in all of this?"

Dr. Julie didn't stop me, instead she just nodded her head. "Go on."

"Because it's like…when me and Shay met George and Carol, it reached a point of no return for me! George and Carol opened up the floodgates when they exposed us to the money. The private parties and private clients! The paid trips n'shit. All'at drove a wedge in between me and Shay, and I was super bitter after that! I went on a rampage, bro."

"And where does *Bonita* fall in all of this? Tell me how what you're involved in now with Bonita correlates to all of this. What pattern or common denominator have you identified with this?"

"The **ménages** chase! If I was never so obsessed with that fantasy, I feel like I woulda never met George and Carol and I woulda never been infatuated with the money aspect. What Sug proposed to me last year…I woulda rejected if it wasn't for that. I wouldn't be tossing and turning at night about it now. Like come on…that's the pattern."

"But Rodney," my therapist reasoned with me. "You said yourself, when you first came back a month ago, that you were stressed out and losing it over *something else*. You explicitly said, 'it's not about the sex'."

"Well, yeah – not *now* it ain't!

"So, what is it about *now*? It's not the wild sex or the fantasies. Your conscience is eating at you lately about these *other* things you've been doing at night."

"I mean, yeah…it's like: chasing *ménages* with Shay led to me chasing *money* with Sug. I'm tripping off *OG Marshall* and *Lorenzo* – all this bullshit beef we done got in behind the hustle. I'm tripping about all the people we stole from – all the people me and Sug deceived. I'm thinking about how my Mama *gotta* be turning over in her grave about me. I'm thinking about my *Pops* and *Grandpa Jerry* – how *at first,* I thought it was the music having a hold on me. Like bro…I went from a college kid to a corporate thug! You know me, Dr. Julie. I'm spinning outta control tryna wrap my head around how I got here. This ain't me."

Dr. Julie kept her eyes locked on me, speaking softly, "I know how difficult it can be to open up like this, Rodney. You're doing good. Keep going."

"It's just so exhausting, man! I really wish I never met that bitch."

"But you *did* meet her, Rodney. And I believe that pinpointing all your recent struggles back to *Bonita* is both unhealthy and deflecting in nature. This is about *you* – *your* choices, *your* triggers, *your* patterns."

"But *that's* the pattern – that's what I'm saying! I know I made mistakes and I know I gotta live with 'em! But my *biggest* mistake has been *trusting* **Sug** when I knew deep down inside, she was toxic for me. I ignored my gut because I was weak in flesh."

"From your experience with Sashé?"

"Right. The ménages and swinger life. Chasing fantasies."

Dr. Julie smirked again, sitting in silence for a few seconds before scribbling on her notepad again. The she suddenly tossed it to the side and leaned in towards me, "Do you wanna know the third thing you tend to do when you've left something out or skipped around intentionally?"

"Sure, Doc," I exhaled deeply, rolling my eyes. "Lay

it on me."

"Now, *this* one is my favorite, Mister Henderson. If I don't notice you staring out that window or drifting off midsentence while rubbing your forehead…it's almost a guarantee that you'll give me this course of action."

"Which is what, man?" I asked irritably. "What do I do?"

"When you really wanna leave something out, you'll start *repeating yourself.* That storytelling brain of yours will reach a point of recognized confusion, not allowing you to move forward. Your mind starts to rebel against you."

I shook my head in defeat, not sure of how to reply, "Man, aight, man. You got it."

"So, what did you leave out?"

"You tell me. You got me all figured out."

Dr. Julie ignored my sarcasm and kept going, "If I had to put my finger on it, I'd say there was something you left out *before* the *Club Ménages* days. Something that sparked this pattern of a path you've been on – but something *non-sexual* in nature. This isn't about the cheating or wild sex…what you've developed with Bonita stems back to something else altogether, my friend."

"Well, are you gonna tell me what that something is?"

"Quite the opposite, Mister Henderson. That's going to be *your* task. And since we're out of time today, you're getting saved by the bell. Your homework before we meet again is to think about what you're trying so desperately in your subconscious to forget about. There was something that *changed* in your life, in your routine that left you in this state of vulnerability and guilt with Bonita. Maybe a relationship or dynamic with someone new, perhaps? *Something* transpired before you got your first taste of ménages and well *before* you met Bonita. I trust that you'll dig deep enough by our next session, Rodney. Just remember – what we're searching for is non-sexual."

I hung my head. These hour-long sessions always go by way too fast. "So now I gotta think about this shit for like 8 days? Like…what the hell, man?"

My therapist stood up and walked to the antique desk behind her chair, reaching for her calendar, "Oh, nonsense! I'm sure you'll figure it out before you even hit the highway! When will you be back in KC again?"

"Next Wednesday," I confirmed, checking my phone as I gathered my things, standing for a stretch.

"I have *Thursday, December 8th, at 11:15am* available. So, I'll see you then?" She then opened her arms for our traditional goodbyes, bringing me in for a big hug before whispering softly, "Be safe on the road, Mister Henderson. *Closure* isn't too far away…"

*   *   *   *   *

…to be continued in TAOC Episodes S2E1

*Have you ever seen a picture or a portrait —
full of beautiful color and intricate detail, so
complex and deep, and exploding with pure
artistry???? Give it but a glance and you'll never
appreciate the true brilliance behind it.
Yet…stare at it for too long….and you'll
become consumed by its mystique and engrossed
to near obsession.*

Cheating is a work of art.

This…

*…is the masterpiece that I've always liked to
call…*

The Art of Cheating

1

<u>September 2007</u>

I took a long gulp out my water bottle...damn near finishing it off. My throat was dry as fukc – that was half of my issue right there. And even though I knew chasing the water with my 'yac wuttin' gon do much to help my cottonmouth, I had to take another sip...*just on the cool.* The *Henny* helps fuel that inner ~~beast~~ energy on the mic. All that was left now was one more deep breath...

Come on – I gotta knock this last verse out so we can wrap this session up early, yo...

Well, let's go then, nigga.

"Aight, bro. I'm ready," I told my engineer. "Run it."

The beat starts playing again in my headphones, and I hear my voice on the end of the hook as I wait to punch in. In a split second, I'm back in character:

"Now why you acting all shy? You know I like to *watch*...
...how ya make it disappear when I hit that spot...
Yeah I'm *deep!* That's why you grabbing them sheets...
I give it to ya from behind like a dog in heat...
Now gone and throw it back at me, yeah, I like it like *that*...
Make it clap...lemme see ya put that arch in ya back...

I'ma – beat it up...round after round...
I know I...got ya sprung when you make that sound...
I hold ya down on my own – I'on *need* no cuffs....
Got my hand 'round ya neck cuz I like to get rough...
(Quit crying!)
Yeah I'm pulling ya hair!!! I know ya sore right *there*...
Go ahead...you can get ya some *air*...
Soon as you get ya breath tho, we gon *fukc* some 'mo...
Put you up against the wall and make you lose control...
Now what's my name?!?! Aye what you *say?!?!*
Yeah that's better, baby...lemme have my way...

LET'S GET DOWN!!!"

"That was the take right there, nigga! Let's go!" ***Jaz***'s voice hit my headphones as he cut the track almost immediately...and I had my headphones off just as quickly.

"Yeah, I'm coming out," I stepped out the booth, feeling myself. Though I wasn't overly excited just yet about doing this music shit...I did have to admit, I *was* getting better at it. I'd only spent about 20 minutes in the booth recording these verses – a year ago I woulda took a full *hour* getting all my vocals done.

Being able to ***focus*** goes a long way.

This time last year, shit was too hectic for me to really concentrate on creating art *outside* of **The Art**. Between me chasing **ménages** and my sister becoming the 8th woman *ever* on the **FBI's** *Top 10 Most Wanted Fugitives* list...I'd went through my fair share of adjusting to bullshit. On the outside looking in, a muhfukca couldn't tell how fukced up I was – but it's no fun dealing with the media putting a bunch of bullshit out there about ya family...and good attorneys don't come cheap. My sister's case was draining the fukc outta me and my people...the fukcin' dicks really had it in for her. Living a normal life had become a challenge…a challenge that I was failing at miserably.

This year, I've found a way to balance it all and get back to *not letting 'em see me sweat.* **Music** has become part of my therapy. This unique way I have with words…this mouthpiece that I'm blessed with – thanks to the beast – I'm finally using it in a way where I can channel all my frustrations creatively. **Grandpa Jerry** would definitely be proud of my dedication, if nothing else. As with anything I put my time and effort behind…once I'm in – I'm *all* in.

Still…for all the talent and potential muhfukcaz tell me my bloodline has – this music shit is mostly an experiment and stress-reliever for me. I can't really see myself making a career outta the shit – if it happens, it happens. The cards were in my favor either way, so I was just running with it.

I was in a good space – with one of my best friends and old college roommates, *Jaz,* making a name for himself as one of the top audio engineers in Kansas City. Watching him build **64111 Studio** from the ground up gave me a front-row view over the years of how the shit works, and I'd been lucky enough to witness some of KC's dopest emcees recording in their rawest element.

On top of that, I'd seen the *business* side of the industry from one of my other best friends and frat brother, **Ricky Rhymes,** with all the work he put in at the radio station with his show *Underground Heat.* Plus, I was already recording voice-overs and writing commercials for *DymeWear, Inc* – the clothing line my frat brother, **Shabba,** was expanding. Writing music seemed to just make sense.

But yet and still, even though I was dedicated with my effort…my real passion still lied elsewhere and deep down, I didn't see it as a long-term thing just yet. In these beginning stages, the music was more so another source for me to transfer some pent up energy.

If I had my way – the perfect scenario would be to see other niggaz I had watched grow as artists in my circle take off, like my brother, **Dell,** and cousin, **Kam**. Hell, even my sister, **Ronnie,** could spit rhymes with the best of 'em. *They* were the rapping muhfukcaz who deserved a shot – not me. But I figured if I went hard at it, some of my energy would be transferred into what they were *already* doing artistically. And if I could get them to get serious about the music from a *business* sense, maybe we could get some *bread* outta the shit. Lord knows we need it.

Everything is all about the **money** right now; this case we fighting in court is way out of our tax bracket. *Money Over Bitchez and Niggaz* became a mantra and way of life and every side hustle has to count. We gotta get this shit however and wherever we can get it. Album and clothing sales wuttin' no overnight thing, though, unfortunately, so during the **Summer** and **Fall of '07** – we all had to be on point with the grind and explore various other ways to keep a steady and quick cash flow.

"Aye, can you bounce that down on disc and just mix it when I leave?" I hollered out at Jaz. "I gotta get down to the barber shop and try to slang these cd's."

Jaz was already fukcin' with the vocals when I sat down in the control room. With his back to me like always, he was locked in and focused on the dual monitors, hard at work, making immediate adjustments. I can't really describe what he was *doing* to the tracks specifically; I didn't understand that *ProTools* shit like he did, and never will.

But I'd watched my nigga teach himself how to record, mix, and master audio since we were college freshmen back at CMSU. We had worked on stepshows, mix cd's, and voice-overs for years together, but never *music* until recently. Honestly, if it wuttin' for Jaz opening up **64111 Studio**, I woulda never even entertained the idea of doing this rap shit.

"Aww, nigga, you 'bout to bounce? We got like a hour and a half left, nigga," he reminded me how much time we had scheduled.

"I know, but shit – I'm tryna make a couple of moves before I head back to Kansas, nigga."

Jaz started to say something in response but was thrown off by loud bass and music coming from the back end of the building. Spinning around in his infamous leather chair, he then hopped up and stormed down the hallway abruptly, leaving me in the control room alone.

"Man, *this* nigga. Aye, **KRUSH!!!** Keep that shit down for a minute, nigga!" he yelled in frustration.

He was screaming at the newest member of *64111*, a young producer who went by the name of **Krush Groove**. Krush was down in his office cooking up some more dopeness as usual; he practically lived at the studio now that he was part of the team. Jaz managed to convince him to take a break for a few minutes, and the two of them walked back in the control room together.

"I see you knocked that bad boy right on out, huh, *HoLLyRod?*" Krush was grinning from ear-to-ear. "How that shit sound so far?"

I only halfway heard him, by the time they had come back to the control room...I was down in my phone – reading my text messages.

Ninety percent of my texts these days were from my main girl, **Sashé**. I had cut down my outside activity almost completely — so if I had texts from anybody else, more than likely it was *business-related*. Today was no different. I scrolled past the two missed texts from random customers at the shop trying to see when I was gonna be up there with my duffle bag. I was programmed at this point to go straight to Sashé's messages *first*, and I had texted her before I went into the booth. Her reply was quick and to the point.

SASHÉ: "Hey love. Oh I'll most def be here when you get home."

Shay was always anxious for me to be home again. After a little over two years, we still couldn't stay away from each other for too long. We've yet to have a serious fight or disagreement...and rarely get on each other's nerves. It's crazy...but we always seem to be on the same positive vibe when we connect — regardless of what's going on outside the house. She's still my *getaway*...my perfect *vacation*.

"What you mean *'so far'*?" Jaz frowned at Krush's comment. "Nigga, this shit *done*, I'm 'bout to mix this shit."

"Aww, that nigga already done? Let me hear that mug, then," Krush replied anxiously.

Again, I *hear* them talking....but I'm only halfway listening in. You know how it is when you locked in on ya phone — I'm trying to be involved in the real world but the *Matrix* got me stuck at the moment. This is some other type of weird, *new territory* — with technology continuing to change and redefine how we communicate and stay engaged on mobile devices. I was still learning how to balance my attention and be in multiple places at once.

Either way, replying to Shay always came first:

ME: "Ok, I'm still at the studio. Are you good? You need anything??"

I looked at the time on my phone as I hit **SEND**. It was now **4:42pm** and my two-hour studio session didn't end 'til 6pm. If I could make it to the barber shop before 5:30, I could prolly make a couple of other moves before leaving *the Missouri side*.

"Wait…what? Hold up – nah, nigga!" I looked up, suddenly realizing what the fellas were saying. "The track ain't done just yet, fam! My *vocals* done but I ain't near done with the *track*, bro."

Jaz was at the computer again, clicking away with his back turned to me, "What else you gotta do to it, nigga? Ricky got something planned for it?"

I stood to dap up Krush before responding, "Nah, nigga. Ricky ain't even heard the beat Krush did for this one – *or* that *last* verse. He don't even know I'm redoing it yet."

"Aight, nigga – don't have that nigga flipping out!!!" Jaz warned me.

"What – this **Ricky Rhymes'** song or some shit?" Krush wondered.

"Nah, bro – I wrote this; it's my song. I just recorded the original version at Rick's house on one of **Indiana Jonez'** beats."

"Yeah – that's Ricky's guy in Chicago," Jaz helped

explain.

"Right, nigga – the nigga who did the beat you had me listen to before I did this one," Krush remembered. "So, what's the deal? You doing a *remix* with my beat?"

"Nah, it's more like a *replacement* n'shit. Something went down at Jonez' lab this summer and now he ain't got the original tracks no more, sooo…"

"Ok – I got you…that's what I'm saying. We redoing it," Krush tilted his head in confirmation. "So, what is this nigga Jaz talking about?"

"Man, you know that nigga on some bullshit," I chuckled.

"Aye, nigga – fukc y'all!!" Jaz snapped back matter-of-factly. "That's between Rod and Ricky. The track dope either way. This nigga talking about he ain't finished with it, though? Man, I'm mixing this shit down, nigga – you tripping."

"Bro, nah man! I ain't done! I still gotta find a chick to ad-lib that muhfukca, bro…bring that shit to life," I stood my ground.

"Man, this nigga," Jaz shook his head again.

"Nah, for real, bro," I continued. "I got a *vision* for it."

Krush laughed at my seriousness, "This nigga tryna be on some ole *'Rico Suave-playboy type'* rapper shit! Who this muhfukca think he is?"

"Nah, boa!!! That nigga Rod, man – I'm telling you! He on some playboy shit in *real life,* nigga!" Jaz corrected his young producer.

"Oh, this nigga got all the hoes, huh, Jaz?" Krush grinned at me, waiting on the punchline.

"Nigga!" Jaz spun around in his chair with the most stern look on his face. "This nigga got *two* bad bitchez at the crib right *now*, that's why he tryna leave early n'shit!"

Jaz was always on my head about how wild I lived. Though most of my close folks hadn't really learned about my *latest* adventures, Jaz was the one nigga I could talk to about almost everything. We practically grew up together since 18. Jaz had seen my entire evolution, way before the **ménages** era. And to this day – he still got a kick outta pointing out the unbelievable shit that seemed to always fall in my lap.

"Man," I shook my head modestly. "Cut that shit out, cuzz!!"

"Am I lying, nigga?!?!" Jaz shot back. "You see dat nigga ain't *disagree*, Krush!"

"Ohhhh, so you saying this nigga HoLLyRod is like the black *Hugh Hefner*, low-key?!?!" Krush's eyes lit up.

"Bro...y'all niggaz, man! Dawg, I'm tryna get to the shop so I can go dump these CD's, nigga!" I fought back the smile. "And I gotta pick up some other money on the way to the crib! Y'all on dat bullshit!"

"Oh, so you *ain't* got two bitchez at the crib, nigga?!?" Jaz turned his lip up with sarcasm. "Ok, cuzz! This nigga wanna be modest today."

I shook my head yet again, "Nah, my girl at the crib...but I don't know where her partner Kris at. I was just texting her now. But, for real, cuzz – I'm just tryna go to the shop, nigga!"

"What you got in the bag, nigga?!" Krush looked down at my feet. "You *Duffle Bag Boy,* too, nigga?!?

"Bro, this nigga get all the new music like two or three weeks before it drops," Jaz kept spilling the beans.

"What?!?!" Krush couldn't believe what he was hearing. "This nigga a fool! What kind of rapper slangs bootleg CD's?!?"

"Aye, nigga, I ain't no rapper – I'm just tryna get money, fool! Fukc the industry…dem niggaz rich and putting out bullshit! Nigga, what you want? You can get *8 for $20* right now, nigga – wassup?!?!"

"Aww, this nigga *bootsy!!!* What you got, nigga?"

I opened my black duffle bag up so Krush could see the hundreds of discs inside. He nearly fell backwards as I then handed him my printed out *inventory list.*

"Nigga!" Krush's jaw dropped.

"Nah, cuzz, he got everything for real," Jaz hollered over my song playing back. "Mixtapes, underground shit, commercial albums."

"Everything but *local* music," I chimed in. "I don't bootleg local artists...fukc that."

I noticed my phone lighting up next to my bag on the couch, which meant Shay was likely texting me back. I kept talking as I picked up the phone to peep her reply. Now that Jaz was talking shit – I *did* start thinking about how things might go later on for me. I wuttin' sure if **Shay** and **Kris** were working at the club tonight, though – they usually came home together anytime they worked the same shift.

"See, that's my bitch right there, nigga...I need to see wassup for later anyway," I boasted arrogantly. "Come on and put that shit on a disc for me so I can jet!!!"

"Shit, it ain't gonna take me long to mix it real quick – it's just your vocals on it," Jaz kept clicking away.

"You ain't even gotta *mix* it; you can wait cuz I still need to find a chick to get on it, bro."

Krush looked up from reading my inventory list, eyebrows raised, "Oh, this nigga was *serious!!!*"

"Nigga, just have one of yo hoes get on the shit," Jaz kept shaking his head in confusion. "Quit bullshitting, nigga!"

"Nah, bro, I ain't got it like that no more," I insisted, sticking to my story about scaling back. "For real...me and my girl play together or not at all these days, my nigga. "

Krush chuckled again, "Damn, nigga – you was serious on *that* shit, *too,* huh?!?!"

"I told you this nigga be on some other shit, cuzz! He got bitchez...don't let him fool you, nigga!" Jaz refused to let up.

"Man, but I ain't got none on deck who 'a hop on this *track*. Not these days, nigga," I glanced down at my phone again. "You know the white girl ain't doing that shit and *Shay* damn sure ain't coming to the lab, nigga!"

"Nigga, so you ain't got *no* other chicks, nigga!?!" Jaz challenged, looking at me with a blank stare. "Nigga, you *know* I know better!"

I paused to look at Shay's reply...making sure I read

11

it right. Suddenly, just that quick, my heart was in my throat...as my eyes widened. This wasn't the reply I was expecting at all...and in fact, this reply was the exact opposite of what would fit here at this exact moment – with all the shit talking going on in the studio about *HoLLyWorld*.

Nonetheless...what Shay texted me helps set up the topic of today's episode that's full of madness. I promise you can't make this shit up.

SASHÉ: "Nope, I don't need anything babe. I'm just sitting here reading all of your text messages in your work phone. I'll see you whenever you get home. You've got some real explaining to do mister..."

"FUKC!!!!!!" I yelled aloud, startling the homies after reading her message twice.

"Wassup, bro?" Jaz's face immediately screwed up, looking at me for an explanation. I just stared at him…but I was really staring *through* him – off into space.

"Wassup, nigga?!?" Krush echoed. "You good???"

"Bro," I hung my head, feeling a lump swelling in my throat. "I fukced up."

"Wassup, nigga?!?!" Jaz repeated himself, eyes open wide. "What that text say?"

I could show him better than I could tell him. As I handed him the phone, I started rubbing my forehead with anxiety....trying to gather my thoughts.

"Awwwww *shit,* nigga! Bro, what's in there, bro?!?" Jaz quickly switched into damage control mode. "Tell me it ain't really shit in there for her to see, bro...come on, cuzz..."

"This nigga just got caught up, bro? *Mr. Playboy???*" Krush was stuck and confused.

"Bro, I don't remember what all is in there. I ain't deleted them messages in a minute," I started rubbing my forehead viciously with my thumb.

"Nigga, you be on creep time on yo *work* phone, bro???" Jaz was still trying to make it make sense.

"Nah, man," I shook my head, staring at my phone again. "I mean...not really...nah. For real! I ain't really been on that shit lately, bro – *on errthang.* I just hope she ain't seen no shit from **Tracy,** bro."

"Who is *Tracy?*" Krush wondered. "One of ya side chicks, nigga??"

"Tra....*Tracy???*" Jaz squinted through his glasses, trying to put a name with a face. "Bro! Is that the outta-town bitch, bro?? You know which one I'm talking about!!!"

"Yeah, bro. That one," my head sank into my chest as my heartbeat sped up.

Jaz hops up out his chair, hollering, "Nigga!!! How you talking to her on yo *work* phone, nigga?? See man, this nigga Rod done started having **ménages** n'shit and getting 'laxed!!!"

"Nah, bro...I ain't been on dat for real, for real! Shit, I don't even remember what all is in there!" I tried to explain, desperately searching my memory. "We only text on that phone when we need a random line before she send something."

"Bro – *who the fukc is Tracy?*" Krush stood up, looking even more confused than before. "This nigga talking about *random lines* n'shit!!! What the fukc you got going on, homie?"

"Nigga, what you bout to tell her, bro???" Jaz asked nervously, disregarding Krush.

"Nigga, I don't know! I gotta figure out what she seen! This shit might get ugly, dawg."

"Oh, so y'all niggaz just gon' *ignore* me n'shit?!" Krush exclaimed loudly.

"Aye bro, you might as well chill for a second...figure this shit out while I work on this record, nigga," Jaz reasoned with me.

"Man....nigga, if **Sashé** see them messages from **Tracy,** bro...."

"Nigga, *who the fukc* is Tracy, *nigga???*" Krush was fed up and demanded to know what all the fuss was about.

Jaz burst out laughing, "Rod, you gotta tell this nigga about ole girl, bro."

"FUKC!!!!" I screamed, nearly at the top of my lungs. My mind was racing as fast as my heart now.

"Yeah, nigga," Krush responded calmly. "I'm curious now."

"Shit, wassup with that *Henn,* nigga??" Jaz turned towards the computer again, craving for a drink.

"It's a half a fifth left," I replied as Jaz's face lit up and he promptly headed out the door to get the *Hennessy* bottle out the booth.

"Aww, shit...you know that nigga ain't playing with that *Henny,* boa," Krush knew what time it was.

"Yeah...I need a few shots while I'm bullshitting," I sighed.

Jaz came back in the room with three red cups, filled with ice. He was already pouring up as I finally started typing my reply to Shay:

ME: "Oh ok lol boo. I'll see you when I get home."

It was important to remain calm at all times. If it was one thing **The Art of Cheating** had taught me in times like these, it was to *never let 'em see me sweat.* You gotta act like everything is all good no matter what. Fortunately, I hadn't experienced *too* many times like these....where I appeared caught with my pants completely down. This was gon' take some real maneuvering to come out of, but I had to remember to maintain my cool.

"Yeah, nigga. You posted up now," Jaz handed us cups and took a sip from his. "Tell this nigga about *Tracy.*

This shit still fukcs me up when I hear it, fam."

Krush started shaking the ice around in his drink, "Yeah, gimme the info! Shit, I might pick up some pointers, nigga – the way you niggaz talking..."

"Aye, let's go in the *smoke room*, cuzz," I urged him, reaching in my pocket for my bag of GG. "I need to roll up, for real."

Krush and I then headed across the hall so I could start breaking the details down and tracing my steps.

"Yeah, that's what I'm talking about, nigga!" Krush smiled, eager to spark up.

"Start at the beginning too, nigga!" Jaz hollered from the other room.

"Aight, 'ole *storybook time* ass nigga! Nah – you know I gotta start at the beginning...that's the only way to tell this story."

Ok. So let's introduce **Tracy**....

*   *   *   *   *

2

So, my nigga Jaz is standing at the vending machine, grabbing some candy as I start schooling Krush on my little secret I've been keeping under wraps.

Again, it's important to note that this was in the *old 64111 Studio,* back in *2007* – *before* the building expansion. Before Jaz started the renovations and moved the main lobby up front, there used to be a small *break room area* where we could blaze up and get creative. I spent a lot of time in that room back in the day, since I never recorded music sober. Sometimes I used to even bring my *vaporizer* in and set up shop, to avoid *smoking* when I had to record. I quickly realized it helped with breathing control if my lungs weren't filled with GG smoke while trying to spit bars in the booth.

Since I was done recording for the day and now suddenly faced with a dilemma...it was time to spark a blunt for old times' sake.

Man, what the fukc could she have seen, bro? We ain't been sloppy like that...

*I don't know, dawg! I mean, you saw what she said, though! She had to see **something**, nigga.*

Yeah, but what, HoLLyRod? We been surgical with this shit lately, bruh. Don't even front...

The beast was right, yo. I had been really fukcin' good lately. But that's why I was so disappointed in myself for slipping up like this. The good thing was – I really *had* changed my cheating habits up, so whatever Shay saw, it couldn't be a call for the death penalty.

But Jaz was *also* right – he knew me well enough to know how I get down. So, when I tell him or anyone else that I got rid of all my bitchez...what that *really* means is that I've stopped talking to chicks that are *easily accessible*. Being able to defeat the addiction that is **The Art of Cheating** starts with getting a hold on the situations you tend to put yourself in.

Like I said earlier, most of my contact outside of Shay these days was business related. There were models I chatted with – but it was always kept super professional. I hadn't really talked to other bi-chicks or been on the prowl since that night I shook **FoXXXy** and we hooked up with Kris this past summer. And even then, I only talked to them chicks online and not through my *phone*.

But when you're a career cheater like myself and you've tried to make a change – it seems like the *cheat gawds* always throw you a *plan B* to keep in your back pocket, in case you ever get weak again. **Fall 2007** was during a rare period of time where everything was all good in my home. Like Jaz was eluding to, I basically had *two pieces of pussy at the crib* to regularly have my way with. Cheating on *that* situation would be ludicrous, right?

Well, **a year ago**, however, I was still *transitioning*, and had a certain situation fall in my lap that I just haven't been able to cut ties with completely. This *'situation'* was a chick named **Tracy**.

"Aight, so I met this chick last year – like right

before my sister went on the run n'shit," I sat down in the smoke room, talking to Krush.

"Damn, nigga! So, y'all been talking for a minute then!" Krush posted up on the opposite end of the couch as I broke the GG down on a notebook. Jaz was standing in the doorway to the hall now, sipping his drink, just smirking.

"Yeah, but check it out," I continued. "The bitch is in *Ohio*."

"This nigga got a outta town side chick!" Krush yelled in disbelief.

"Nah, just keep listening," Jaz cut in. "Let him tell this story, nigga…"

*　　*　　*　　*　　*

<u>*Late July 2006*</u>

So, I'm online one night, searching for prey – just a few months after me and Shay tried to do the *ménage* with her best friend **Kourtney**. This was the beginning of my first hunting period and I was busy at work. Shay and I had just agreed that it was okay for me to fukc other chicks, as long as the three of us got down together.

Remember, I thought it would be a piece of cake at first. All I had to do was find another sexy chick and my whole world would never be the same. Well, as y'all know by now, that's much easier said than done – and this was where I first started experiencing the frustrating side of the search…just two months in on the hunt.

Bro, I can see now – it's gon take some real focus for me to get to the point that Shay wants me to be at...where I'm not doing anything sneaky or outta bounds at all.

No shit, Sherlock! Cuz I'm bout ready to fukc one of these hoes without Shay ass! Come on, nigga – fukc this bullshit!

After searching on *AdultFriendFinder*, *MySpace*, or even *Rude.com* for a couple of hours – I'd be sitting on the computer with a hard dick, gawking at all the profiles and endless pics of half-naked hoes. One thing would lead to another and I'd find myself up to no good – looking for chicks who wuttin' necessarily bi or into couples.

I just couldn't help myself. So, most of the time when I started to stray...I would try to limit it to *'cyber-sex'* and not entertain really getting to know a bitch or trying to meet outside of internet chatting. Well, it wuttin' always that easy…so, of course, I had some flings here and there.

This one night in particular, though, I received a private message on *MySpace* that proved to be a pivotal, cornerstone moment in my **Art of Cheating** legacy.

So I'm at home by myself, as I normally was during that time. I remember it being hot as fukc outside and I had went to the pool for a quick dip before sitting down in front of my computer for a couple of hours. I was still in my trunks and towel at the time I got this **Inbox**:

BuckeyeGirl216: "Hello Mr Kumfort-her. How are you this evening?"

The_Kumfort-her: "Hey there. I'm chilling and you??"

It all started off so innocent; so normal. Perhaps the normalcy is what kept me talking that first night. This was sort of the end of my *vanilla lifestyle* days, without me fully *realizing* those days were numbered. Whatever the case was, Tracy and I ended up in a long conversation and talked for an hour or so.

She was from the suburb area of Cleveland...just far enough away where she couldn't get me in trouble with Shay. But honestly, when Tracy and I started chatting, it really *was* on some friendly shit and didn't involve flirting or sex-related chats – like not at *all* in the beginning. There was once upon a time in the cyber world where you really *could* just make casual conversation with a random person and it wasn't considered creepy. This best describes how **Tracy** came into the picture. It was just friendly small talk at first.

The_Kumfort-her: "Yeah I been here most my life but I was born in Saint Louis..."

BuckeyeGirl216: "Oh that's nice. I have never been to Missouri, I have a friend who grew up there though. Have you ever been to Ohio?"

The_Kumfort-her: "Nope, been lots of places but not in your neck of the woods. I hear it gets cold lol."

Buckeye Girl216: "Lol yes that is true. It's not bad this time of year tho. So what do you like to do for fun? Are you online a lot?"

The_Kumfort-her: "Lately I have been lol...but for the most part I'm a laid back cat, I'm into reading a lot. And writing."

BuckeyeGirl216: "Oh really? What do you write? I love to read!"

So anyway, Tracy and I talk about absolutely nothing important for a little while before she tells me that she gotta take off and enjoyed our chat. I ain't really think much of it. But then the next day *(and pretty much every day after that)* she sends me another **Inbox** message, each day sparking a new conversation. We never talked about anything really important, so she became just a new *online friend* that lived in another state.

The conversations were so vanilla that I never even had the opportunity to hide my relationship with Shay from her. Tracy never even *asked* if I had a woman or if I was single. At the time, I was *technically single* – Sashé and I wuttin' calling ourselves a couple officially just yet. But the *point* is – Tracy really wuttin' asking me about my personal dating life and neither was I when it came to her. It's important for me to keep reiterating that as I retrace my steps…because things with Tracy did start to change rather quickly from where they started. And even now, it's still hard for me to pinpoint exactly *how* the sudden changes happened.

Damn, is that always the case?

Stay focused, Rod…

*   *   *   *   *

August 2006

Ok. So anyway, it's about a month after Tracy and I first started chatting. I check my **Inbox** before heading to work and see a message from my Ohio friend telling me to hit her up ASAP. She says she really needs to talk to somebody and can't think of anyone else she can vent to. At the time that I checked my messages, she wuttin' currently logged in.

So, without thinking twice, _(and because I'm actually a cool guy underneath all the arrogant, belligerent, egotistical bullshit)_ I shoot her a message with my _phone number_ attached, telling her she can text me if I'm not logged on whenever she receives _my_ reply.

She texts me maybe an hour later, and though I didn't recognize the number, I knew it was her because I wuttin' talking to nobody from the _OHIO_ area. So, as soon as she texts me, I saved her name in my phone.

TRACY: "Hey there, are you busy?"

ME: "Hey you. No, I'm not. Wassup? Are you good? Talk to me..."

TRACY: "No. I'm really not. I'm not good at all. Sorry to bother you, but I don't have anyone else to talk to. I think I'm gonna lose my mind!"

Uh oh. This don't sound good.

Man I'on even know why you keep talking to that girl anyway, nigga! She ain't even no freak!

Man, chill out — it ain't like that with Tracy. She said she need a shoulder and we bored at work anyway. Relax right quick…

ME: "Ok. Calm down. Talk to me. What happened?"

TRACY: "I've been in tears all day, I haven't had sleep at all. My mother died last night."

My heart instantly sank as I let out a long sigh. I know all too well how devastating losing a mother can be. And anytime the thought crosses my mind, I get instantly triggered. I get reminded of all the horrors Ronnie and I faced, my emotions forced into turmoil. So, almost instinctively…my sympathy went out to Tracy for her loss.

ME: "Omg Tracy! I am so sorry to hear that! I lost my mom to cancer when I was 14, I'm so sorry. How did she pass?"

TRACY: "She had breast cancer. She's been sick for a while, I just never imagined it would be this soon. I remembered you told me how you *lost your mom...how on earth did you deal with this? I don't think I am going to make it!"*

ME: "I am so sorry you're going through this. It's not easy for me, even to this day. I don't know how I've made it this far...I guess I just refused to give up. How is your family taking it?"

TRACY: "My dad is taking it very hard. They were really close. I can tell it's tearing him apart. Rodney, it really hurts so much."

ME: "I know it does. Trust me I know."

TRACY: "I wish you were here to hug me right now. The tears won't stop rolling.
ME: "I would give you a big, tight hug if I was! I'm so sorry. If there's anything else I can do - let me know. However I can help."

TRACY: "Just keep talking to me, please?? I feel a little better with you texting me back, I don't have anyone else to talk to right now."

We texted back and forth for the rest of the night, and then everyday leading up to the funeral. It never felt like I was *cheating* on Shay for it. I mean, I can't really explain *why*, but I kinda felt compelled to help console Tracy over that shit. And plus, I knew talking to me made her feel better. It wuttin' too much for me to just text her back and forth during her time of grieving. Right?

So, over the next few weeks, I became Tracy's cyber shoulder to cry on…

*   *   *   *   *

September 2006

Labor Day weekend came around and Ronnie went on the run from the police. It's no secret what came next. My sister was wanted for murder, amidst a city-wide gang war. That meant I was now forced to quickly change up my routine when it came to the extracurricular activities. As a result, I ended up not responding to a few of Tracy's texts over the span of a couple of weeks.

It wuttin' on purpose or nothing. My focus and attention just started to wrap around helping my sister get shit in order before they caught up with her. But as with any female, when you don't give them your undivided attention – they start taking that shit *personal.* Tracy took that real personal.

I was leaving this meeting with **Pete Patrick**, the attorney we were considering hiring for Ronnie's case, when I received this super long text. The message was one of those *'Sorry to keep bothering you – I wish you the best'* type of joints. I was already frustrated from the meeting at the lawyer's office, but I could tell Tracy's feelings were really hurt from not hearing from me for a few weeks. I decided to respond by opening up a little bit – something I really never did with folks I barely knew.

ME: "Hey Tracy. Listen don't feel like that,

you weren't a burden or bothering me. I've just been going through some things of my own here lately with my family."

TRACY: "Oh my God - what's wrong??? What happened? Is everyone ok?"

ME: "No one died or got hurt, it's not like that. It's kind of complicated, hard to talk about actual."

TRACY: "You can talk to me Rodney. Don't shut me out. What is it?"

ME: "Well it's my sister. They're flashing her on the news all over Kansas City right now. She's wanted for murder."

TRACY: "Oh wow! Oh my God! What the heck happened??? Is she locked up?"

ME: "Hell no, she's not turning herself in. And I don't really know the full story, I just left a meeting with the lawyer. This shit is stressing me the fukc out."

TRACY: "I can only imagine. Your family leans on you because you're such a strong spirit. But what happens when you need to lean on a shoulder?"

ME: "I know huh? This shit is crazy! I have no idea where I'm gonna come up with all this money to help pay for the attorney, but ain't no way we doing the public defender thing. Fukc that."

TRACY: "No! You all cannot use a public defender, trust me - that's just a setup. How much is the case going to cost?"

ME: "Shit, he normally charges $25K for that type shit, it's 2nd degree murder. But he said he'll take 20k if we promise to pay him. It's the retainer upfront shit that we need to come up with in the meantime. I don't know man. This shit is crazy."

TRACY: "How much to get him retained?"

ME: "He needs 2500 to start. Maybe I'll rob a fukcin' bank smh.."

TRACY: "Rodney! Don't you ever talk like that again! If you go to jail, then who will look out for your brothers & sister??? Please don't say things like that!"

ME: "I'm only half serious. I'm just saying. that's a lot of money to come up with."

TRACY: "That's actually not a bad price, do

you think he's worth it?"

ME: "Yeah. Pete's the only criminal defense attorney in the state to ever win a Federal case. He's definitely worth it."

TRACY: "Let me make some calls. If I can send you the 2500, will you promise not to do anything stupid?"

Hold up...what she say, nigga?

Man, she can't be serious, dawg. Nah, man.

Nigga, she bet not be!

ME: "What? Lol stop playing girl!!!! Now isn't the time. I really need to figure this out."

TRACY: "Rodney. I'm serious. I need a few hours to get it together...but you need to promise me you won't do anything stupid in the meantime and get yourself in trouble."

ME: "Ok...you for real?? Like seriously for real???"

TRACY: "Yes. I am serious. I want to help

you Rodney."

ME: "But why?? You've never even met me."

TRACY: "True. And honesty I don't know if it's the best idea or not but you need help. And you helped me out more than you know when my mom passed. I feel like I have to help you if I can."

ME: "Ok but you don't have to. I helped you get through it cuz it was the right thing to do."

TRACY: "And so is this. Rodney let me make some calls and I will text you back shortly. Just promise you won't do anything 'til u hear back from me, ok?"

*   *   *   *   *

September 2007

Krush just stared at me with his beady eyes…waiting on me to crack a smile. But I was serious as a heart attack and just getting started. This Tracy story only gets crazier.

"I told you, nigga," Jaz broke the brief silence. "This shit is unreal!"

"So what happened, nigga? Did she really send the cheese? Nigga, you gotta be fukcin' with me!" Krush started flooding me with questions.

Jaz then noticed my cup was low and started pouring me another drink. The *Henny* bottle was nearly empty.

"Bro, I wouldn't be sitting here wasting time with y'all niggaz just making up shit! This is real talk, my nigga!"

"Aye, pause that shit for a minute," Jaz interrupted. "We need to go grab some more *Henn*."

"I think the vatos still open across the street, I'll run over there, bro," Krush stood up. "Keep this nigga here. I gotta hear how this shit played out."

Jaz smirked, handing Krush some cash, "This nigga ain't going nowhere. He still gotta figure out what to do with his girl, nigga."

Speaking of which – I was already beyond nervous about this shit with Shay, especially after recalling how me and Tracy had started off. But my anxiety got even worse as I looked down at Shay's latest text, sent five minutes ago:

SASHÉ: "Yeah. You might wanna take your time and get your story together because this won't be easy to shrug off. You forget you've taught me a thing or 2 about sneaking around..."

"Aye Krush, nigga!!!" I yelled as he grabbed his car keys. "Hurry back with that *Henny!* Like yesterday!!"

*   *   *   *   *

3

Hennessy at ***64111 Studio*** was like part of a ritual. Jaz was a real drinker and also one of the main reasons I appreciated good quality liquor. We had been drinking partners dating as far back as the late ***90's.*** Now that we were doing business and working together as adults – the pouring up was way more serious. Our studio sessions were now filled with *Henny*, brew, and non-stop, sarcastic belligerence. We would take shots, cuss at each other, and fight like brothers for hours…but we always made magic and got shit done in the midst of the bafoolery.

It couldn't happen without the *Hennessy*. The 'yac was the gas that kept the engine running. We were older and more seasoned now, but with the same nostalgic energy from back in the dorms when I was setting ***campus records***.

A few years younger than us, ***Krush*** was new to the squad and I felt like he needed to get indoctrinated accordingly. He was a smaller dude who wasn't a big drinker. Jaz didn't think Krush could handle the type of weed I was blowing, but I knew he was more of a GG man like myself. And since Jaz didn't smoke and these niggaz were technically holding me hostage to tell this story, *somebody* had to blaze up with me while I sorted this shit through.

Right now I could care less about Jaz preferring his producer not to smoke on the job. Krush was gon learn today.

"Shit, I'm already high," he tried to wave me off. I still held my hand out, passing Krush the *Swisher* as Jaz sat in the control room for a few minutes – working on my track again.

My voice sounded dope as fukc on *Krush Groove* beats. I was really buzzing now, slightly more calm than I was before with the scary texts from Sashé. I'm sure the fact that I hadn't looked at my phone in the last twenty minutes had as much to do with my more composed state as my beloved GG did, though.

"Nah, fukc that, nigga," I blew a cloud into the air. "We smoking. Hit this shit, boa."

Jaz shouted from the other room, "That nigga gon pass out, yo! Watch what I tell ya."

"Shut up fool – you the nigga scared to hit the blunt!" Krush shot back, now feeling pressured enough to take the tree out my hand.

"That nigga gon smoke with me, too, one day, Krush! Don't even trip!"

"Yeah right, nigga! Not near!" Jaz disagreed like he always did.

"Yeah, that nigga a hoe," Krush puffed on the blunt. "Nah, but for real, nigga...get back to this story."

"Nigga, I forgot where I was at..."

"Nigga, you was on ya way to pick up that bread!" Jaz yelled again.

"Damn, bitch ass nigga – don't spoil it!" Krush snapped at him, coughing up smoke.

"Fukc that shit! That nigga need to get to the good part and quit bullshitting!"

"You already knew I got that money from her, though, cuzz," I hushed Jaz up before taking the blunt from Krush again. "It's *how* it happened that makes the shit crazy."

*   *   *   *   *

<u>September 2006</u>

Tracy advised me to expect a *Money Gram* the following Friday. I mean, I can't lie, I ain't really believe it was gon happen; the whole idea was a bit outrageous.

Like…come on, man. So, it's a chick in Ohio, who I ain't never met, all of a sudden 'bout to send me money for Ronnie's lawyer???

Ain't no need to overthink it, bruh.

I'm just saying – on what planet does shit like this happen? Even in HoLLyWorld the shit is unheard of, dawg!

Just try not to fukc this up, brodie! Let it play out – trust me on this one…

Now let's just keep shit in perspective here for a second. The fact that a bitch wanted to give me money wuttin' the shocker. Nah…not at all. That notion was actually quite common; I done received plenty of tokens of appreciation from women I've blessed over the years. If you fukc with a bitch the right way, she'll wanna look out for you. She'll, in fact, feel *compelled* to take care of you, in

one way or another, if you leave the right impression –
this is simply the science of the **Son's Curse**.

It also wuttin' that surprising that a bitch I never *met*
before would send me bread. The summer before I met
Sashé, for instance, there was **Kitty**, the bitch from St.
Louis who I was *cyber pimpin'* the long-distance way. But
Kitty was a slut whore bitch – another freak I'd met
online on some sex-chat shit. The bitch was so intrigued
by how I came at her with the cyber-sex that she was
quickly willing to do *whatever* else I told her, just based off
my pure *'Daddy'* energy.

The Art of Cheating teaches us to vocalize our
boldest demands with confidence and entitlement. But I'd
be lying if I said when I asked *Kitty* if she'd really *sell pussy*
through a *text* that I knew she'd *go* for it. I had never *met*
that bitch, never had a chance to put this **HoLLyWooD**
on her. I guess she thought my word game was doper than
anything she'd ever experienced thus far. And it *was* crazy
to me, at first, when she really started calling me for
guidance on *how to get paid to fukc*. But after that first time
she put money in my bank account – it almost felt like it
was no big deal. Kitty told me I was *Daddy*…so it made
sense she saw fit to *treat* me as such.

This **Tracy** situation was different from Kitty,
though. With Kitty, we were talking *sex* from the get-go.
And with all of this happening after **The HooKup** with
Tianna, Kitty got me at a time when I was just getting to
know my inner **beast**. The sexual chats with Kitty were of a
more dominant nature on my end; she couldn't help but
feel that Daddy energy early on. And Kitty *called* me often
– just about every time she was pulling up on money, I
listened to her over the *phone* until it was all good. Kitty
was also trying to *meet up* from the beginning. We almost
had a **ménage** with **Sassy** and *would have* if Sassy hadn't
disappeared by the time I finally *did* fukc Kitty.

But interactions with *Tracy* were through *text only* and we weren't having conversations of a sexual or even *flirtatious* nature. If Tracy wanted to help me, I believed she was sincerely doing it out of the kindness of her heart. And *that* part of the equation was fukcin' me up. No one had ever done shit like that for me before. Especially not a woman. In all my prior experiences, I woulda had to at least entertain the thought of breaking her back before a bitch would even think about breaking me off.

Bro, and what type of bitch can just come up with a couple racks to spare in a couple of days...just like that?

You overthinking again, Rod...

These are valid ass questions, nigga! How much do we really know about this chick?

You know her moms died recently...maybe she left her some money, nigga!

But why spend it on me??? A couple racks is a still a couple racks, bruh!

Unless she left her millions, nigga!
But even still — why would she be blowing that type of money on some nigga she met on **MySpace** *miles away? I mean...who the fukc **is** this chick? Is she somebody important?*

Nigga, I don't know! She ain't told us much, like you just said. But who the fukc cares, nigga?!

I think her pops might be somebody important cuz she always talking about going to meetings with him — like she gotta schedule appointments with his secretary...

Well, nigga, is HE loaded? Shit . . . maybe that's the case . . .

I mean – I really don't know. I ain't even sure what the fukc **she** really do for a living either, though! She say she work in a hospital; long shifts, long hours. You ain't tripping off all the times when she act like she can't access her phone at work, nigga?

Nigga, I could care less about all'at shit! She tryna kick us down and I say we let her, nigga!

But, bro. The more that I think about it – how can we prove that anything she tells us is true?

I've only seen a few pics of this chick. Sure, this is **2006** and a vast majority of folks ain't got camera phones or webcams on their computers yet – but I still wuttin' 100% sure of what this chick even *looked* like.

Man, you really can't just let this shit play out, nigga?

Nigga, for all we know, them pics she emailed a while back might not even be her!

Bro, I swear if you fukc this up . . .

Man, nigga I know you think it's crazy we ain't talked about no freaky shit at **all**, dawg! Stop fronting, cuzz!

Most muhfukcaz I met in the cyber world woulda *been* showed their freaky side by now, but Tracy hadn't went there. I mean, I guess I hadn't either, for that matter. But I had my reasons, though – right?

I was trying to turn over a new leaf and show some

restraint. If Tracy was closer...it woulda been much harder. From the pics, she was most definitely fukcable...if that was indeed her. She was a heavier build, but not sloppy or obese. Her skin tone was lighter – caramel-colored like Shay. Huge tits. I'd definitely hit if it came down to it. But, like I said, we hadn't even gone halfway there with the texts.

And then, literally, texting was our **only** form of communication! This shit was for real unheard of. We had been talking for two months and all contact had been through fukcin' text messaging!

I guess I *could* use that to my advantage, though. With me and Shay getting more serious, it was important that things stayed discreet with Tracy. Sashé didn't need to know I had a new text friend and I couldn't let Tracy find out I had a chick I was seeing. Or did that even *matter*?

I mean...I was used to playing situations like these by the rules of **The Art of Cheating**, but would Tracy even *care* if I had a chick with what she was offering?

Damn, bro – what if Tracy got a dude and **she** *on some* **Art of Cheating** *shit her-damn-self?*

Maaaan....gimme a fukcin' break, Rod! Just let this shit play out, bro...

*　　*　　*　　*　　*

Everything was so up in the air. So, I was skeptical as fukc on my way home from work that Friday night, waiting on Tracy to text me confirmation that the funds were sent.

41

6pm came around and I hadn't talked to her since around noon, when she had a few moments to text on her break. She told me that she was gon' send the *Money Gram* after she got off work at 7pm my time. With an hour to spare…I had just enough time to figure out how I would shake Sashé to go pick up the money. I needed to get this done without attracting any attention.

Shay was spending the weekend at my spot and had drove up from the Burg earlier that day as soon as she was done with class. When I walked in the apartment, she was watching tv in the living room…sprawled out on the couch in panties and one of my *Denver Broncos* t-shirts.

"Hey, you," her voice was soft and gentle as always. She didn't get up. Instead, she twisted around and sat up on her knees with her arms stretched…waiting on my embrace.

"Hey. Whatchu in here doing??" I took her in my arms, squeezing firmly. The burgundy couch cover suddenly came undone as our bodies shifted, exposing the dingy cream colored sofa underneath. I really needed to get new furniture.

"Waiting on you," she responded, almost whining. "It took forever for you to get off! My gosh!"

"Oh, stop. It took me six minutes to get home."

"Ok, but still! I *missed* you," she was still hugging me tightly, as if she hadn't seen me in weeks. I guess it had been a few days.

"I missed you, too," I told her, moaning as I pulled her in closer.

Shay grinded her hips against me as I stood. "Hmmmm…you have missed me," she whispered, pulling my shirt up and reaching down in my *Dockers* to tug on my dick.

I was instantly rock hard in her small hands and it made her lick her lips. Before I could beat her to it...she then started unbuckling my belt, pulling my pants down. My boxer briefs fell to the floor with my slacks, and my throbbing **wooD** flopped out in front of her face. She started licking on the head slowly...letting drool drip out of her mouth and down her chin before she started sucking the tip.

"Damn, Shay," my knees buckled. "Fukc."

Shay had some great sex and her pussy stayed amazingly tight. Wet as fukc. Super tight. Dripping. Leaking down her legs, wetting mine up. And did I mention – it was *airtight* snug? Yeah, Shay had that *good-good*. And no matter who you are or what other plans you might have had prior – when you get a taste of that good-good after a long day of light work...you tend to doze off after that nice, long nut...

*　　*　　*　　*　　*

When I woke up it was **8:27pm** and I had damn near – *just that quick* – forgot about what was supposed to be going down with *Tracy*. I hopped up from the living room floor quickly after making out the time on the cable box. I started looking for my phone as I glanced at Shay, who was knocked out on the floor ass-naked, right in the same spot I had knocked her down.

But as soon as she felt me get up and start moving around, she called out for me, "Daddy...where you going??"

I didn't respond right away, since I was already

staring down at my phone at the missed messages from Tracy. Her last one read:

TRACY: "Well I guess you don't need my help anymore. Please at least respond and let me know you're ok."

Fukc!

See, nigga! I told yo ass!

I couldn't type fast enough, fumbling my phone as I shook my head:

ME: "My bad, my battery died...I just got home. I'm ok, just let me know when you are ready."

Sashé was still calling for me as I stood by the computer desk in the darkness. She was clearly anxious for me to come back and lay with her longer, "Baaabe...where are you??"

"I'm right here, baby. Hold on."

"Can we go lay in the bedroom??" she asked, her voice drifting off. I looked back down at my phone, as Tracy had already replied.

Damn, that was fast!

Good, nigga! Now don't mess this shit up for us. Just follow my lead.

TRACY: "Mmm hmm. You probably just got outta some pussy. It's cool...I see how it is."

Well, damn. That's a first.

ME: "Lol what? No. I wish. I ain't had none in forever."

TRACY: "Oh yeah sure...tell me anything. I don't believe that. Not with how handsome you are. You have females throwing themselves at you, I'm sure."

Man, what the hell?? She ain't never talked like this...

So what, bro? Just go along with it! Play it for what it's worth so she can still do what she said she would, nigga.

ME: "Oh stop it. I'm just an average nigga. I ain't special."

TRACY: "Well I definitely disagree there.

I'm on my way to send your money now, about 15 minutes away. Do you have a Money Gram close to you?"

ME: "Yeah they close at 9 or 10 I think. I'll go ahead and leave now if you're close."

TRACY: "Ok, I'll text you when I get there. I need you to do me a favor though."

ME: "Ok...what's the deal?"
TRACY: "I'll tell you when I get close. Let me finish driving."

ME: "Ok, talk to you in a minute."

Ok, bet! It look like it's really going down, my nigga!

Right! Now I just need to figure out how to shake this girl for a few minutes so I can go pick it up.

Shay had finally managed to get up off the floor and was stumbling towards me, half sleep and still whining, "Baaaabe…can we go lay in the bed now???"

She was tugging on my arm, just like a little kid. This was my chance. If I could lay her down real quick...I could run to the Walmart nearby and be back before she fully woke up.

"Yeah, boo. I need to run to the store first, though.

I'll be right back."

Suddenly, it was like she got pinched. In a split second, Shay then snapped out of her half-sleep state, and was wide awake, "Awww, maaan!!! Babe! Ok, well I'm riding with you."

Before I had even heard the words entirely, she was already darting back into the living room. looking for her clothes. I mumbled under my breath in frustration and screwed my face up. She turned the lights on and I wuttin' sure she seen the look on my face before I played it off. Either way...I had to play it cool. No reason to panic. She was more than likely gon stay in the car if I told her I just needed to run in. This was still doable.

Or, at least I *thought* so before we left. Once we were in the car a few minutes later...I thought to look at my phone to see if Tracy had hit me up again and indeed she had.

TRACY: "Hey, I'm almost there. Are you on your way?"

ME: "Yeah...I'm pulling up in a minute. In the car now."

TRACY: "Ok so are you gonna do me this favor before I go in?"

ME: "Yeah sure - anything. What you need me to do?"

TRACY: "I want you to call me so I can

finally hear your voice."

Shit.

ME: "Call you? Right now??"

TRACY: "Yes! I wanna hear your voice! Just for a few minutes before I send it. Is that a problem???"

I glanced over at Shay in the passenger seat and then quickly back in my phone, biting my lip in contemplation.

Fukc man! Now how the hell is this shit supposed to work???

*   *   *   *   *

4

<u>September 2007</u>

Krush glanced at Jaz as if I was joking, before spewing in my direction, "Nigga, get the fukc outta here! So, what happened, nigga? Did you call her or what??"

We were back in the control room now. Jaz was done mixing my vocals, and converting the audio to burn to disc. I was sitting on the far left side of the room, in a chair cater-cornered, shaking my head and smirking.

"Man, bro, listen! The way you gotta play this shit, ain't no room for no fumbles! Like straight up, no matter what – you can't be out here dropping balls!"

The *Henny* mixed with GG had activated my passion, the cockiness and belligerence starting to show. I could hear it all in my voice and I knew that's what Jaz was laughing at, "Dat nigga feeling himself now!"

"Jaz, what the fukc this nigga talking about?? I'm saying – did you call the bitch or what?"

"Bro, but this bitch really in *Ohio*, though," Jaz kept harping away.

"Nigga!" I bit my lip, snapping back to my current reality. "I know I ain't leave no muhfukcin' messages in that phone from Tracy, bro! I think I know what Shay mighta saw. But I don't know, man...at the same time, I just don't think I left none of Tracy's shit in there. I'm almost positive, bro."

"You think or you *know*, nigga?!" Krush raised his eyebrow.

"Bro, I'm almost *sure,* for real!

"When the last time you used that work phone, nigga?" Jaz wondered. "How often you be on that one?"

His question made me cringe, "Nigga, I gotta get to the *crib,* bro!"

"So, y'all live together n'shit??" Krush probed, trying to lighten the mood a bit.

"Shit, basically. She been at my crib since she graduated in May," I told him. "We bout to move in *officially* to this bigger spot in like a couple of weeks."

"This nigga found this dope ass spot in *Overland Park* – killing shit, though!" Jaz started bragging for me.

"Big baller ass nigga!" Krush's face lit up. "I see why you got bitchez sending you money n'shit, nigga – them muhfukcin' *bills!*"

"Damn, Rod! Nigga, how the fukc you ain't erased messages?!?" Jaz's mood shifted again, remembering my situation. "See?! Told you – nigga you getting too relaxed..."

"I know, bro...I know. I'm tripping!" I couldn't disagree. "But nigga, she never even glances at that phone! What the fukc, bro?!? That's why I usually take errthang with me – my dumb ass thinking she ain't paying attention n'shit!"

"And nigga, you know she *know* how you get down! This nigga was helping Shay cheat on her dude when they first met, nigga!" Jaz turned to Krush again.

"What, nigga?!?! What kind of shit??"

"Bro, I'm telling you," Jaz continued in jest. "This nigga be on some wild shit.

"Man, fukc that! I'm trying to hear the rest of this story, nigga – wassup???" Krush had finally had enough and was ready to hear more.

"Y'all niggaz got me late to the shop n'shit, nigga! It's already damn near 5:30!" I shook my head, knowing the longer I stalled, the worse shit might get.

"Nigga, finish telling this nigga what happened," Jaz ignored my worries, keeping the pressure on. "Quit bullshitting!"

I was looking down at my phone again as he tried to persuade me. Shay hadn't texted me back in a minute – but for whatever reason, I wuttin' super nervous about it. I was still completely shell-shocked that she was actually going through my phone, though. Especially that fukcin' work phone. We had been through some wild shit over these last couple of years and, in a weird way, the trust between us was much stronger than any of my previous situations – in spite of the fact that Shay and I started off as mutual *cheaters*.

Sitting here at the studio backtracking is some profound shit for me, as now I'm reminded that me and my ex, **KeLLy**, started off the *same* way – on some *creeping* shit. There's a clear pattern in how my affairs tend to start and I'm not sure what it means. Maybe I should talk to my *therapist* about it. But at any rate, I *do* know that the level of trust between Sashé and I is *deep* – deeper than anything I've had before.

I mean, it's crazy. For all these lessons I've learned about how to get away with shit, Sashé has always made me bend the rules. I ignored so many of 'em when we first met.

Sometimes I still can't believe I actually fell in love with my mistress chick, and left KeLLy in the cold so heartless like I did. I knew it was wrong and a true cardinal sin in the **Art**…but dammit, man. I just really couldn't help myself with Shay. I'm realizing now how vulnerable I am with her. How she not only makes me *think* outside of the norm, but even encourages me to *act* outside of it. I'm a different person altogether with Shay – which is why shit like this *work phone incident* is happening today.

I woulda *never* done this shit with KeLLy. The sloppiest I ever got with Kells was when Shay came in the picture. More and more, though, I'm starting to not even *count* that. Because I mean, hey – that was essentially the end of me and Kells anyway. At the *height* of our toxic relationship, there's no way I woulda been *this* 'laxed. I'm letting my guard down in a major way with Shay, to the point where I'm acting like an *average* cheater.

And again. It's not that I'm *out here* like I used to be. But still, I had to admit – I *had* been sneaky on my work phone lately.

What can I say? I still get weak. I still have this need to have multiple women in my life – it's what I'm used to. Lemme be clear – this last year has been *lovely*. Ever since we hooked up with Kris, I've been having some of the best sex in life. If I thought Shay was a nympho who couldn't get enough, her Russian partner in crime, Kris, was just as bad.

Kristina still considered herself *straight*, but she was totally gay for Sashé. I'm starting to notice that dynamic more commonly with chicks and their BFFs the closer we get to the end of *'07*. These girls out here all be getting freaky with their friends on the low. And Shay and Kris were getting close as hell…even closer than Shay was with *Kourtney* when I thought about it. I couldn't be in a better place – in a circle of trust that never comes this easily.

But still, there was *something* missing…

Sashé wasn't the *hood chick* I was used to having around; she was more white-girl than Kris sometimes. Sure, we had a dope connection, but Shay spoke more to the *square* in me – she couldn't really relate to my darker roots.

Now don't get me wrong. This never got in the way of what we had. We had grown into something beautiful with the way we balanced each other out.

But *still. Something* was off-balance…

Every once in a while, I got that itch to be around a bitch who can roll a blunt for a nigga. You know what I mean – the type of chick who didn't watch *Grey's Anatomy*. Of course, KeLLy didn't roll blunts *or* smoke but she wuttin' *green* like Sashé. I mean, Kells could *at least* quote old episodes of *Martin* with me. It's selfishly wild how I was missing that shit lately – but being around Shay and Kris these last few months really made me miss the hood.

Technically, I wuttin' tryna *cheat*, though. My sexual cravings were *more* than taken care of. There was just that small, pecky void calling for attention lately.

So, here's what I'm thinking Shay mighta seen in my work phone:

I had decided the best fix to my urge would be to find a chick on some *'smoke buddy'* type shit – a more edgy chick I could just lay up and be a *nigga* around. But since Ronnie was locked up, I had to be on *quarantine* status. Part of the reason I moved out to *Overland Park, KS* with the white folks was to keep me outta the line of any crossfire from my folks' beef around the inner city. I was only traveling in and out of **the Missouri side** on business; all work and no play. But if I could find a chick in the city who I could trust, just on some homegirl shit, I felt like it would be enough to satisfy my *hood energy* cravings.

So, a few weeks back, I had started texting a couple of potentials *from my work phone*...feeling them out. I normally didn't use that bulky ass *Motorola* for anything other than sales-related shit for the gig. More than likely, I left some evidence in there related to my *smoke buddy search*. But every once in a while, **Tracy** would also text that work number, in code, from a different Ohio phone line to be discreet.

I knew I was slipping up leaving my work phone at home with Sashé hanging around unsupervised. I know I slipped up even *more* by not *erasing* messages recently. But man, it's just been a minute since I was deep off painting in **The Art**. I just didn't think Shay would start *looking* for shit...with how smooth things have been between us.

Staring at my phone these few seconds in silence, I know one thing is for certain. I pray to the *cheat gawds* that it wuttin' any messages from *Tracy* that Shay saw. I almost *wish* that she saw the messages with the smoke buddy potentials instead. That would be the lesser of the two evils and I can get outta that shit *no problem*.

Nonetheless, I know I gotta face the music with Sashé either way when I leave this studio today. Retracing my steps with the homies is crucial right now…

"Aight, dawg," I took a deep breath, gathering myself. "For real, this what I'm saying. When niggaz be on sneaky shit...like *most* niggaz do – it's just *some* shit you *cannot* fukcin' get caught doing, bruh. I'm talmbout – you gotta be willing to run through *hell and high water* to keep that shit under control. Treat that shit like you might do some time if that shit hit the fan. **The Art of Cheating** ain't to be played with…"

*   *   *   *   *

<u>September 2006</u>

Shay was still half sleep in the car…but she was *in* the damn car, nonetheless.

Man it ain't no damn way I can call this Tracy chick with Shay sitting right here! Fukc, man.

I don't know why you ain't just creep out real quick on her ass, nigga!

Fukc! This dat bullshit!

Nigga, if you don't call that bitch, though, she might not send that fukcin' money!

I know…I know, bro. Lemme at least text her back.

ME: "Ok, hold on, lemme park."

That should buy me a couple minutes. I mean, I really *was* getting ready to park, pulling into the *Walmart Supercenter* parking lot. Quickly, I started trying to figure out how I'm gon' convince Shay to stay in the car so I could handle this shit.

But then Tracy texted me back two minutes later...as I finished backing the car in:

TRACY: "Ok hurry!"

"Bitch, hurry up and send that bread..." my beast's patience was wearing dangerously thin.

"You staying in the car?" I looked over at Shay, hoping she was too exhausted to do otherwise.

"I don't know, babe," she turned her head slowly, eyes low.

"You might as well, babe. I'll be right back." I moved swiftly, before she could react. She was in slow motion; she tripped. Quicker than you could clear ya throat, I was outta the car and walking rapidly towards the entrance...not looking back. I already had my phone in hand by the time I walked inside, Tracy's line ringing twice before the automatic doors closed behind me.

Damn, why the hell she ain't picking right up?

The voicemail chimed in as I approached the

Customer Service counter, *"Hello, you have reached Tracy Evanston, please leave a message."*

What the fukc, man?

See? She playing...

That's when I suddenly realize that I'm just standing here without no confirmation or reference number or *nothing* for the *Money Gram,* "Maaaaan. What the hell am I doing, man?"

The chubby white guy at the desk looks up at me with a confused expression, "I'm sorry, sir?"

"Nah, my bad, bro – talking to myself," I explained apologetically.
"Can I help you?" he asked with obvious impatience.

"Yeah, gimme a second. I'll be ready in a minute."

Unless I won't...

I started to turn red in the face when my phone finally rang in my hand.

Ok, here we go.

'Bout damn time!

I took a deep breath, remembering to stay calm, "Hello?"

"Hey, what's up?" she sounded preppy and innocent; not quite like Shay cuz Tracy was a little older. But then ironically – Tracy's voice was a little more high-pitched. She actually sounded *younger*.

"Shit...nothing. I'm here at the place now," I told her.

"Ok, good. I'm standing in line. Are you okay? You sound tired."

"Nah, I'm good. I always sound like this."

Tracy giggled on the other end, "Really?? Ok, I have to get used to it – you like to *text* so much! I'm sorry."

"No need to apologize," I noticed the desk clerk staring me down. "It's cool."

"I just didn't know what to expect – you know?" she continued. "Your voice is really nice, though."

"Right on, that's wassup. You don't sound too bad yaself!"

"Thank you. You're making me blush, Rodney!"

"What I say?"

"Nothing," she sounded flustered. "Your voice is deep."

I let out a light chuckle, "I'm saying – is that a *bad* thing?"

"Not at all," she lowered her voice, nearly to a flirtatious whisper. "You know most women like a manly man."

"Is that right?" I quickly followed suit as my phone started beeping on the other end. I knew who it was before even looking.

Shay in the car getting anxious, nigga!!!

She'll be aight! Keep Miss Buckeye talking...

"Yeah. I'm next in line now," Tracy switched gears. "Are there a lot of people in line where you are?"

"Nah," my voice drifted off, hearing the line beep again. "Hold on for a minute. Don't hang up."

I then clicked over hastily, taking my voice up a notch, "Hello???"

"Are you at the register, Daddy??" she sounded annoyed, but still soft and sweet. "What the heck is taking so long???"

"I'll be out in a minute, Shay baby," I matched her tone, disarming myself. "What's wrong?"

"Nothing. I just miss you," she replied with mischief. "It's kinda cold out here. Hurry up."

"I didn't leave the keys in the car?"

"Nooo...I don't know. Wait," she stopped. "Did you??"

Dammit, Shay...

Come on, cuzz...

I heard another beep in my ear, this time for an incoming text message. I also noticed the desk clerk had disappeared as I took the phone away from my ear to see who texted.

TRACY: "Guess you had to go. Talk to you later."

Fukc!!! This can't be happening!

Sashé's laughter sounded off in the phone, "Oh, babe! Wait – you *did!* They're right here, you left the car running for me!"

"Ok, babe. Turn the heat on. I'll be out soon," I couldn't get the words outta my mouth quick enough.

I then hit the **END** button several times to make sure it hung up and called Tracy back immediately.

No answer. Three rings before the voicemail.

Almost feeling desperate...I called her right back.

Same thing. Three rings and a voicemail…

"Fukc me, man!!" I cried out in the middle of the store.

"Can I help you, sir?!??" the clerk had suddenly showed up again, clearly tired of waiting on me.

Damn, where the fukc he come from again?

"My bad, bro," I fought hard to keep my cool, reminding myself it's not his fault. "My bad..."

"I'm shutting down in five minutes, sir – if you need some help."

Fukc, man! What time is it???

Just then I received another text message:

TRACY: "You should be able to use your ID but the reference # is 42750163."

Oh shit! She did it!

Jackpot, nigga!!!

"Nah, bro...I'm ready," I told the nerdy looking clerk. "Here I come." I rushed over to the counter, reaching for my ID in my pocket.

"Great, what can I help you with?"

"I need to pick up a *Money Gram.*"

"Ok sir, I'll need your driver's license. And do you happen to know how much you're receiving?"

I handed him my ID, "Yeah. It's twenty-five hundred."

He takes my ID and starts typing in the computer, fast as fukc. He must really be ready to get off work. I start texting Tracy back as he looks for the transfer.

ME: "Hey, I just tried to call back, I didn't mean to leave you on hold."

I hope she ain't mad or tripping.

Nigga, she can't be too mad if she sent that cheese, right? Fukc it! We in there now.

Yeah, but I still gotta show concern, right?

TRACY: "It's fine. Did u get your money?"

ME: "He's looking it up now."

The clerk then looks up at me, with that same confused ass look on his face that's starting to low-key piss me off, "Sir, I don't have a transfer in your name for that amount. Do you know when it was sent?"

What the fukc is this nigga talking about?

"Yeah, it was sent a few minutes ago, bro," I bit my lip, trying to keep the ~~beast~~ at bay.

"Oh, well it can typically take up to ten minutes to finish processing," the white-boy clerk explained. "The systems will be shutting down in a couple of minutes, though."

Bullshit they will!!!!

Yeah, nah!!! I need this money now!!!

I had already scheduled a meeting with the attorney in the morning, and he was making a special stop at his office to sit down with me.

"Nah, come on, bro," I started reasoning with him. "Check that shit again. Here...I have a reference number. I'll write it down."

"Okay, yes – because typically you're supposed to fill out this form with all of that info."

Nigga, typically you supposed to explain all'at shit when I first state my business — hoe ass nigga! Don't get typically slapped!

"Aight, bro. Well, *you* work here...not me. Can you look up this reference number, please? Thanks."

He searches in the computer a few more seconds, then glances up to his left at the clock on the wall.

This muthafukca really irking me right now, bro...

"Ok, sir are you sure you have the right info?" the clerk asked again.

"What you mean, bro?" my frustration was showing now. "That's the info, it should be in there! What's the problem??"

"Oh, there's no problem, sir," he insisted. "I pulled up the *transfer*. It's just not the *amount* you said it was. I'm just making sure this is right."

Say what now???

"Hold on. Say *what* now?"

"Yes," the clerk nodded his head in confirmation. "I do have a transfer in here under your name. But it's for *one thousand dollars* in US currency."

"Nah, bro. You need to check that again. It should be 2500."

"Sir, this is the only one I have under your name in the system. It's for *one thousand.* Do you want to cash it out or no? I need to lock my register up."

Maaaaaaan...come on man!!!!

*   *   *   *   *

5

I can't remember how many times I called Tracy's phone after only getting that rack instead of the $2500 – but I must've stood there for another ten minutes or so, blowing her shit up. I was livid.

Why the fukc would she not do what the fukc she said she was doing?!?!

See, this is the type of shit that make me fly off the deep end – I told you not to fukc this up, nigga!

I knew it was too good to be true! She need to pick up this muhfukcin' phone – I know she see me calling!

Her phone kept going to voicemail but at that point it didn't matter anyway. The cornball ass clerk had shut down his register and got ghost. And I ain't know of another *Money Gram* pickup location that might be open later anyway – *if* it just so happened to be a mistake on Tracy's behalf.

Walking back out to the car, somehow I knew it wuttin' a mistake, though. And I didn't have the patience to even deal with that train of thought. If it's one thing I couldn't stand – it's when a bitch say she gon' do some shit and go back on her word. I'm so muthafukcin' pissed right now, I could punch somebody.

I take a deep breath before getting back in the car…trying to hide my rage from Shay. She's talking on her phone when I open the door and barely even notices when I hop in.

"I know!!! They make it seem like it's just sooo easy!!"

What the hell is she talking about?

Who is she even talking to?

Man, I'm irritated as fukc right now, bro.

Whoever she was talking to, they were keeping her pre-occupied as I rode back to the apartment in silence — with the biggest attitude in Kansas…and *$1000* more in my pocket than the *$30* I left home with.

*   *   *   *   *

September 2006
10:12pm

Yeah I know, I know — *what is there to complain about?*

Not many niggaz I knew had bitchez they never met

sending 'em cash. I only knew of one – the same nigga narrating this episode.

I mean, come on now. I had a dope ass spot, a nice, clean ride, and a walk-in closet full of *SuperFLY* shit. On top of all'at...I was laid up with a superfreak baddie who only wanted dick from me.

Really...I shouldn't complain.

Man, nah – fukc that bullshit! Shit ain't always sweet as it seems – you know we needed every penny that she promised!!!

Man, I'm trying not to think about it. But you right, big dawg.

If Tracy wuttin' really planning on sending what she said, she shoulda just said that shit!

And it's not that I'm ungrateful. I just had plans for that money, bro.

Tracy knew that shit. If I was anywhere near that bitch right now, I'd choke the shit outta her.

*Nah, for real...I prolly wouldn't go there with it. But I might at least **throw** some shit at the wall.*

Nigga, while you bullshitting you need to figure out what to tell the attorney! You know this ain't gon' be enough to get Pete on board.

What the fukc, man?!?!

I needed to calm down, so I got up outta bed with sleeping Sashé and went into the front room. After I fired

up my vaporizer to get elevated, I grabbed a controller
and turned on my **PS2** so I could try to blow off some
steam. Video games always helped take my mind off shit
and since Shay was knocked out, a head-to-head **Madden**
game sounded like the perfect distraction.

Mid-November couldn't come soon enough,
though. Sony was finally launching the new **PlayStation 3**
in a few weeks and I had already taken vacation so I could
sit overnight in line for the new console. I wuttin' fukcin'
around. When the **PS2** was released back in **2000**, I waited
in line at *Walmart* in the Burg for three days straight with
my ship, **J Dub**. I couldn't wait for that new shit to come
out; copping on release date was a tradition for me.

I think what was killing me the most about Tracy
shorting me was the fact that the whole situation was
something I hadn't talked to anyone else about yet. I
mean, there was so much I was uncertain about the whole
ordeal that it was almost embarrassing.

And who *could* I talk to besides my conscience
anyway about the shit?? None of the *Nupes* would believe
the shit, and if I mentioned this to **Ricky** he was sure to
talk to me in such a way that I would just be done with
Tracy altogether. **Jaz** and I were close...but this Tracy
situation was still too new for me to give him enough
details to really help talk me through it.

I also knew my hood homies Dell and Kam
wouldn't be much help with this. Them niggaz was barely
even sold on the whole idea of the **texting** game at this
point – they'd think this type of shit was borderline
weirdo activity. I mean, let's be real. I'm technically
involved in a *text-only relationship* with an *outta towner*. This
type of shit just didn't happen in our world. I was
completely on my own with this one and it was killing me
thus far.

I was in the 2nd quarter of a close game when I finally got a text reply from Tracy. The time on the clock was *10:48pm.*

TRACY: "Did u get your money? My phone died."

Oh wow. Really?

Really, bitch??

I stared at the phone for a few seconds out the corner of my eye, unsure about how to respond.

How she just gon hit me back all of a sudden like everything just copacetic?!?

What the fukc, man???

I waited 'til halftime before I finally replied...turning my phone on vibrate so Shay couldn't hear any of the notifications in the other room.

ME: "Whatever. U play too fukcin' much!"

I was still fuming mad. After about three more

minutes, she sent another message:

TRACY: *"So you didn't get it? I sent it Rodney."*

ME: *"No u didn't! You didn't send what you said you would!"*

TRACY: *"Well that was your fault."*

ME: *"My fault??? What the fukc man??? You on some bullshit!!!"*

TRACY: *"Stop cussing at me Rodney! I don't like you talking to me like that. I'm not on BS. That's you."*

I nearly dropped my phone on the floor...fingers moving fast as ever. I could hear the delay of game penalties on my abandoned *PlayStation* game and wuttin' worried about getting kicked offline. I needed to speak my mind to this stranger playing friend.

ME: *"How am I on bullshit? Wtf?!?! I ain't did shit! You sent $1000! What happened to the $2500????"*

TRACY: *"Why did you leave me on hold???"*

ME: "What??? I clicked back over and u hung up!!! I called u back 20 times! So that's why you didn't send the whole 25???"

TRACY: "I don't like being left on hold, that's rude. I'm not one of those little silly chicks you're used to Rodney."

ME: "Man wtf are you talking about?!?! See. you on some bullshit!!!"

TRACY: "See, you're still cussing at me. I'll just talk to you later when you calm down."

Nigga, don't you hate when muhfukcaz doing everything in dey power to make you lose yo cool and they got the nerve to not acknowledge that you ain't even snapped yet?!?! You better get this bitch before I do, bruh...

ME: "Oh wow. Wow Tracy. Ok. You played me."

TRACY: "Really? I played you?!?! I just sent you $1000!!! Ungrateful. You're playing me!"

ME: "Playing you??? Playing you how??? Wtf Tracy?!?!?"

Bro, I have no idea what she talking about! She really pissing me off!

TRACY: "You think I'm stupid???"

ME: "I'm starting to. You acting dumb as fukc right now man."

TRACY: "I'm not a dummy either. I've done my homework on u, I know more than u think."

What the hell is she talking about, bruh???

Dawg, I'm about two seconds from just saying 'fukc it'!!! Is all of this dumb shit even worth the rack she sent me??

Well, I ain't say all'at, nigga...

Cuz what is this even about? What is she getting at?

Ain't no way she could know about Sashé. She talmbout some homework n 'shit...

Fukc, man! See, that's what I'm saying, bro! We really don't know who this bitch is in real life, nigga!

ME: "Tracy what are you talking about,

man? I don't have time for these games!!!!

TRACY: "I'm not a man and I do not play games!"

ME: "You know what I mean!!' U playing fukcin' games! I ain't got time go..."

TRACY: "You don't have time for me, but you give time to those broke KC bitchez??"

Man, where is all of this coming from??!?

Why she acting like we even talk like this?!?!

ME: "What bitchez are you talking about? I don't fukc with no 'broke' bitchez!! Why are you trying to turn this around on me when you lied about having the money?!?! Get the fukc outta here!!!"

TRACY: "Yea ok lol. I didn't LIE. Trust me, the money is nothing. I could pay the whole 25k if I wanted to. You need to realize who u are talking to like this. I've never been rude to you. Next time don't keep me on hold for your little broke bitch."

The confidence in the tone of her text made me bite my lip. Ain't no bitch ever talked to me like this. And my dominant ~~beast~~ always feels cause to react with even more dominance when challenged.

You bet not let this muhfukca get away with coming at us this strong, nigga! The fukc?!

But what the fukc I'm 'sposed to say to that? Especially when it's making my dick hard. You like that shit, nigga.

As I wrestled with my thoughts, before I could figure out my comeback, Tracy then follows up with:

TRACY: "And trust me, those little girls you deal with are broke. You just don't know any better."

ME: "Fukc you."

Seriously? That's all you got, nigga?

That's all I got, nigga. She on a roll right now...

TRACY: "You're lucky I can't right now."

ME: "Bitch YOU lucky I can't right now."

TRACY: "Don't talk to me like that. Why can't you? Because of your girlfriend?"

ME: "What girlfriend are you talking about Tracy?"

TRACY: "I don't know her name, but if you want me to find out I can. Answer my question."

ME: "What question? Becuz you not here, you in Ohio, that's why. Why you coming at me like this all of a sudden?"
TRACY: "Somebody needs to take charge in this situation & u are under too much stress. I'm flying to Missouri in the morning. Come spend the night with me."

Just when I thought I was almost catching up to where all this might be going, she hit me with *that* shit.

What exactly the fukc is she on right now???

Nigga, clearly she want the dick! She ain't skipping all the guessing games and throwing that out there for nothing, nigga. You know the Code...

I mean, I know this dick 'a make her act right, too. That actually might not be a bad idea, while you bullshitting...

It 'a at least balance this thing out on our end, bruh. We ain't had this advantage otherwise.

Yeah, but I mean, damn! She just gon' up and say, 'meet **tomorrow***? Man, hell nah! That type of shit gotta be planned out, you know that…*

ME: "Tomorrow?? Nah…I can't do tomorrow, that's too soon. U just talking shit."

TRACY: "I'm serious. I will be in Saint Louis for 3 days with a friend of mine. That's not far from u like Cleveland is."

Why is she **just** *now telling me this? Is she testing me??*

ME: "What? Really? Why are you just now telling me you bout to be in my state?"

TRACY: "Would it have mattered if u knew sooner? You're not interested in me like that!"

ME: "How do u know that?"

TRACY: "Like I said, I'm not stupid. If you wanted me, I would know it."

ME: "You just think u know everything.

That's your problem."

TRACY: "Prove me wrong. I will rent you a car so you don't have to put miles on yours. Come spend the weekend with me."

ME: "I just told u I can't do tomorrow."

TRACY: "Like I thought."

ME: "Whatever, it ain't like that - I have to work! I can't just take off?"

TRACY: "Ok Rodney: Stick to that story."

I looked up from my phone, shaking my head. I ain't know what else to really say to her at this point.

I mean, I wish the bitch would've just told me this offer came with special terms n'shit!! We coulda avoided all of this bullshit in the first place!!!

Yeah, she on some other shit, bro. I ain't gon' lie. It's almost like she TRYING to blow the spot...

That's what I'm saying — is all this even worth it at this point, nigga?

Ok, but maybe we should try to get one more payday out the deal, Rod...

Man, fukc that. I bout to take my winnings and leave this muhfukcin' table while I'm ahead, nigga! I'm 'bout to block this bipolar bitch…

ME: "How the fukc can u get mad after u just played me on that money??! Then u expect me to just up & come see u in St Louis on short notice just like that??? U are something else, man. I thought u really wanted to help me! If this was about u getting ur rocks off wit me you coulda just said that to a nigga! I thought this was something different – but this is why I don't let people get close to me, I shoulda known better. Goodbye Tracy."

Fukc it, I need to shut it down for the night and just keep it moving. So, I tossed my phone to the side as it made a slight thump, bouncing on the couch. Then after I got up to power off my **PlayStation**, I stood in front of the tv…drifting off in more thought.

I told you it was just too much not adding up with this chick, bro. I really need to just let it go.

I don't know, dawg. We mighta overreacted just a tad bit…

Man, nah. It already seemed too good to be true, nigga. This little exchange was just confirmation.

Yeah, but what if it wuttin', Rod? Just hear me out…

*No, nigga! I need to snap outta this dream world you got me caught up in, dawg. Nothing in life ever comes this easy. Just like with the **ménages**…*

Aye, but the ménages shit seem like it might work out one day! Who's to say the same shit can't happen with Tracy, fam?

Maaan…fukc that. In the end, this Tracy bitch is just another female thirsty for a nigga, and she can't compete with my situation with Shay. The risk ain't even worth all this back and forth! I gotta stay focused.

Dawg, Shay ain't gon find out about this chick, bruh! Let it play out…

No, nigga! It's too many holes in it and I got enough unclear shit on my plate right now as it is.

Just one more, brodie…

Fukc that bitch.

I got so lost in my thoughts that I ain't even flinch when I heard my phone vibrate again on the couch behind me. I instantly knew it was another text from Tracy but I wuttin' even tryna read that shit right now. Maybe not ever.

My dick was rock hard and curved to the left in my shorts. Suddenly all I could think about as I stood there was that sweet, wet pussy sitting in between Shay's slim thighs in my bedroom. How I was gon' stare at it when I opened her legs up as she slept; how I was gon' kiss her clit hood real softly with a light pecker of preparation. I liked to *lick* Shay's pussy more than *suck* on it. Light flickers always take her over the top. You had to take your time to make Sashé cum, indulge in every moment and never rush the flow.

I'm standing now, thinking about it so hard that when I heard her voice behind me, I nearly jump outta my skin.

"Babe, they're texting you back."

I turned around to find her standing there naked with my cell phone in her hand. My heart skipped a beat and I instinctively moved towards her with swiftness, taking her left hand in my right. Her right arm then fell to her side with my phone and I pulled her close to me by the waist, so she couldn't look down at the device.

"Damn, baby. You scared me," I spoke in the most soothing voice. "How long you been standing there?"

"I'm sorry, Daddy," Shay rubbed her face against my shoulder. "I woke up and you were gone."

"You must've felt me thinking about you," I replied seductively.

Sashé stood on her toes to kiss me on my neck, and I grabbed her ass cheeks with both hands. My breathing was heavy with common nervousness and horny, lustful anxiousness.

"I did," she whispered.

"You feel that, too?" I asked as we grinded our hips together in unison.

Her pussy felt warmer than usual. "Hmmmm, do *you* feel that?" she bit her lip. Her hands were all over my bare chest, my phone now missing.

"Damn, girl," my knees buckled as Shay reached down in my shorts, knowing that was the key to getting her way right now. My dick jumped up in anticipation, thumping against her palm.

"Let's go back to bed, Daddy…"

Yeah. Let's.

*　　　*　　　*　　　*　　　*

8:42am

After another long night of fluid swapping with Sashé…I woke up feeling refreshed and recharged. She was already up and out of bed, and I could smell her cooking breakfast in the kitchen.

Damn.

That shit 'bout to be right on time, nigga.

I was scheduled to meet with Ronnie's attorney at 10:45am and couldn't remember if I told Shay that or not. My mind had been all over the place. As I sat on the edge of the bed to gather my thoughts, I also couldn't remember if I had told **Tracy** about the scheduled Saturday morning meeting.

Well, we know she damn sure she was the only one we told about the down payment. And the only one who broke that promise to help out.

Right! Then the bitch had the nerve to try to turn it around on me — like she was really tripping off me putting her on hold!

Stupid ass bitch.

See, man? I'm 'bout to get mad all over again now that it's all coming back to me…

Nah, remember you already went off and said ya piece last night, nigga. Don't even trip.

Yeah, you right. Bitch, I'm HoLLyRod — I ain't got time for sometimey ass hoes! That's her loss…not mine.

I stood up to stretch and do that morning yawn to officially kick the day off. That's when I suddenly remembered how Tracy *did* text me back after my rant reply last night. I remembered how I hadn't even looked at my phone when it vibrated…how Shay had been standing there telling me I had a new text.

Shit.

WHERE IS MY PHONE?!?!?!?

I hit the living room within seconds, going through the bathroom so I didn't have to pass through the kitchen.

Fukc! How long have I been out with Shay up and moving around?

Man, that'll be just our luck if she saw those damn messages from Tracy!!!

*And it ain't no lock on my phone or **nothing** to stop her from picking it up and being nosy. I shoulda **been** saved Tracy's name under something else, nigga! Fukc, bro!!!*

Stay cool, Rod. Never let 'em see you sweat...

As I darted out the bathroom into the living room, I immediately noticed the phone wuttin' on the floor *or* the couch. The couch covers were uneven again and I couldn't remember if I left 'em like that last night or what. I musta vaped damn near a blunt's worth of GG when I got out of bed last night. My memory wuttin' coming back to me fast enough.

Sashé was in the kitchen at the stove, her back facing me. She still hadn't seen or heard me, so as I straightened the burgundy covers on the couch...I glanced around frantically for my phone – scanning the room.

Dawg, I don't see that shit nowhere!

Not a good sign. Not a good sign, Rod...

Ok, Ok. Think...think, Rodney...

At least go test the waters, nigga.

I gulped and slowly walked up behind Shay, "Good morning, baby."

"Babe!" she nearly dropped the spatula. "You scared me!"

"I'm sorry, my bad," I embraced her tightly, grinning. "Well, now we're even."

"Don't do that, babe!" she kept whining. "I could've burned you with grease!"

"What are you cooking?"

"I'm making us chicken omelettes and fried potatoes. You're supposed to be still in bed!"

"No, I needed to get up," I stepped back and glanced around. "Have you seen my phone?"

"Uhm, yes. I put it in there on the nightstand for you," she rolled her eyes. "It's been going off all dang morning!"

Dammit!

I tried to play off how quickly I moved away from Shay to head back to the bedroom, but I knew it was nothing more than a nice try. I had no idea how I ain't notice the damn phone right on the nightstand but once I reached it, I heard it vibrating again with yet *another* new text message.

Scrolling quickly – I barely paid attention to the message from my cousin, **Benny**, but I made a mental note to read his coded message as soon as the coast was clear. More than likely Benny was texting me about Ronnie. I needed to make sure there were no 'read' messages from Tracy, though. Shay wuttin' acting like she went through my phone...but aye, you never know.

Until you DO.

I had several other new message notifications prior to the latest from my cousin Benny. But there was only *one* from Tracy – the same message from *last night*.

I could now see it was a stream of multiple messages she sent at *11:58pm*, still marked unread and broken up in bunches:

TRACY: "Rodney wait. Don't say goodbye like that. Ok. I'm sorry. You're mad. I'm mad – we both are saying mean things to each other out of frustrations. I may have overreacted to u leaving me on hold, and I know I act spoiled. My father tells me that all of the time.

"..Ok you're right – the trip is short notice so that would upset me as well. I'm just used to having my way, and I want to be close to u like others have the chance to be. Accept my apology please Rodney.

"..It's not easy being the only child your whole life and then somebody like u comes along

and I can't have my way. I just thought we were getting to know each other better and I got upset as I found myself liking u more. Please don't be mad. I will make it up to u when I get back to Ohio, I promise..

"..I will send the rest when I get back to Ohio next week. Just promise me you will still be my friend and talk to me. I want us to be closer. I want to meet u, and I will respect your time as I want u to respect mine. ok?

"..If I make the arrangements will u meet me in Miami before I go to NY in 2 weeks? The weekend of 10/13...just for the weekend - just me and you. You need to get away from all of that stress anyway, let me help you Rodney. I promise to make all of this up to u if u let me. Say you will."

I stared at all the texts in awe, now in even more disbelief than I was the night before.

You still wanna block this chick, nigga?

Uhmmmm....on second thought, my nigga — this shit might not be so easy to walk away from after all...

*　　*　　*　　*　　*

6

**September 2007**

Krush's face was screwed up, looking at me like I was clinical, "Nigga, you crazy! I'd 'a been on that plane in a heartbeat, nigga!"

"That's what I told this nigga!" Jaz agreed, turning his lip up. "This nigga talmbout he ain't know what to do!"

So, what'd you end up doing, nigga?"

Now don't ask me where I learned this cuz I couldn't tell you in one simple answer. Throughout the years, I've learned the game from multiple mentors and experiences. But it's more truth to this shit than the promise of death after life.

The blood cells of *pimpin'* run through everyone's veins. Some have a very low concentration of these cells, while others seem to naturally extract the magic from 'em. Many say it can either be *cultivated* or *stunted from growth* at an early age. I suppose it does start at the core.

At any rate, you end up having three types of people in this dark and taboo lifestyle empowered by **The Art**: **pimps**, **whores**, and **tricks**. Well before we all start fukcin', we each start to fall into one or more of these categories. The powerful energy of sex forces it on us. Let's break it down.

"

The **whore** refers to your sexual prowess. Hormones are crazy – right? We all can have a little bit of whore in us. I mean, who *doesn't* like sex? Who doesn't want to be the biggest freak in the world when they get it in?

Whether you're behind closed doors with the one you love and trust or just slutting it out with whoever made you horny that night – it's all the same. The freak in you comes from that human desire that needs to be fulfilled, and those urges can be dangerous for anyone to manage. There's an inner **whore** living in us all – one that you've either learned how to tame or completely lost control of.

Time is money…since both share the ability to be *spent.* You can choose to spend frugally or lavishly; either making *wise decisions* or being *carefree* in your habits. The older you get, the more one becomes more valuable to you than the other. Comparing **time vs money** can be a little tricky, however. Time is something you can't get back, but then again, money doesn't grow on trees.

Now, stay with me here. How you start to look at **time vs money** is *directly* related to which category of person you ultimately fall under.

These concepts apply to both male and female. We're all humans looking for companionship from another – somebody to let our inner **whore** be free with. Some of us become willing to spend **time** chasing our fantasies...the rest of us are more inclined to spend more **money** and less **time**. Then you have those who are willing to trick off both **time** *and* **money**.

It's still **trickin'** if you got it. **Trickin'** is simply another word for *spending.* You can have all the **time** and **money** in the world to spend – you're still **trickin'** it off if you ain't *getting it back.*

94

To get it *back* is **pimpin'**. When you can somehow find a way to **pimp** the situation for more than it's worth — for *more than what you've invested* into it — *that's* where the separation of **pimpin'** vs **trickin'** takes place.

The mentality is complex. Even a **pimp** is a **whore** at times. But then sometimes a **pimp** can *also* be a **trick**. The key is the **pimp** learns how to get more than what he bargained for overall. The **pimp** understands and can appreciate the motives behind the **whoring** and **trickin'**. He knows how to tame the **whore** urges and he realizes you gotta be able to manage what makes one human. When the return on the investment outweighs the **time** or **money** you **tricked** off to get what you were after, suddenly it's not **trickin'** after all.

The **pimp** understands this is simply SCIENCE. But on the *contrary* — to get to that point is *easier said than done*.

Many of us either end up being **tricks** or **whoring** with little to nothing in return. This is especially true in **The Art of Cheating**. As a cheater, when it's all said and done, you out here just fukcin' around with nothing to show for it but crazy memories.

Unless you really fukcin' good at what you do.

When you really good at what you do and you truly understand how the game really works — you *walk* like a, *talk* like a, *cheat* like a **pimp**.

*And I was **really** fukcin' good at what I did...*

"Man, bro," I shook my head at the fellas as they waited impatiently for more of the story. "I promise I ain't mean to get on this shit like this, bruh."

Jaz pointed at me with his red cup, "See, there you go with that bullshit, nigga..."

"For real, bro," I insisted.

"Man, nigga, I still wanna call bullshit, too!" Krush started ranting. "This bitch barely know you and talking about flying you out on *trips* n'shit, nigga?! For what? Put me on, nigga. I need to know how you got that off, bruh. Is he making this shit up, Jaz?"

"Bro. Sashé bought this nigga a **Xbox 360** like right after they met, nigga!" Jaz started bringing up old shit.

"Yeah right, nigga," Krush wasn't convinced by any means.

"It was for Christmas, though," I shrugged, taking another sip of 'yac.

"The nigga barely even play that shit!" Jaz shook his head in envy.

"Aww, you be on that **PlayStation?"** Krush smirked and I could feel his gamer energy.

"Yeah, that's my shit, nigga." I nodded in agreement.

Jaz hopped outta his chair, bumping the table next to him, nearly knocking the *Hennessy* bottle to the floor. He was in my face, drunk and turned all the way up, screaming, "Nigga that bitch in Ohio bought you that **PS3**, didn't she???!"

I just burst out laughing, unable to object before Jaz and Krush started screaming like *Kobe* had just dunked on somebody again in the *Finals*. There was so much more to this **Tracy** situation than I had ever talked about. So much more to weigh in on....

These niggaz just don't know.

But, see the thing is – even when it comes damn near natural and you're really fukcin' good at what you do, this shit is *still* **The Art of Cheating**.

Nothing ever comes as easy as it seems…

*   *   *   *   *

<u>January 2007</u>

This bitch play too much, nigga. For real. That's all I'm saying.

So, what I'm saying ain't true?

I ain't saying that, nigga…I'm saying…

Man, just go see what she sent and quit being paranoid!

After dealing with Tracy for almost four months, I'm still torn about being done with this situation. It's crazy how the universe works. I had been trying my best for the last *year* to cut off any distractions that could potentially ruin my chances at a ménage with Shay. I had made some good strides that I definitely deserved credit for...but somehow I always find myself back at it. These cyber temptations had me in a chokehold.

I was having a hard enough time with not pressing the issue with **FoXXXy**, the freaky chick I met on *AdultFriendFinder* a few months before Tracy crossed my internet path. Our online chats were still going steady and strong…but I gave myself a pat on the back for simply maintaining at least a little bit of self-control. After all, *FoXXXy* was only a few miles away. Keeping my beast at bay was definitely a challenge, but at the same time, FoXXXy was tempting me with *sex* and I was used to that.

Tracy was moving different. Even with all the bs she stayed on, the fact that she was using **money** instead of sex to keep me coming back made it hard to walk away with no hesitation. This was new territory for me…and an even newer form of enticing the beast.

Now that it's the weekend before my 28th birthday, I'm starting to get used to this back and forth with my inner beast about the constant back and forth with my online secret from Ohio.

I've learned a helluva lot more about her since she shorted me that first time – some of it verified and some of it just the story she kept sticking to. But either way, our interactions were no longer nice and sweet. Apparently that was just *cyber foreplay*. Over the last three months, I had finally gotten to know the *real* Tracy…the entitled, only child, prima donna ass bitch that she was.

The chick was definitely *paid* – that much I was able to confirm above anything else. Tracy was sitting on some serious bank and wuttin' being shy anymore about putting it out there. I still ain't know exactly where her cash flow came from, though. The bitch talked about investments and property management like she was really out here handling business. She was always on a trip somewhere for some reason – at times unreachable.

Every once in a while she now contacts me from a random number with a different area code – just to let me know she was getting my texts, promising she'll get back to me.

Oh, and get *this*: sometimes I get contacted by her *maid* – this Jamaican bitch named **Henrietta** with a strong accent. When Tracy sends me money or needs to get a message to me, she'll have Henrietta call with *Money Gram* reference numbers or info.

I thought it was all just a bunch of babybakc bullshit…but the bitch wouldn't let me walk away. Anytime I went too long without responding, she hit me with the guilt trips and monetary gifts. In exchange, I gave her my time and attention until she pissed me off…then it all started over again.

Hiding this shit from Sashé had been a challenge, but not as hard as it would've been before my reformation process. As the days passed, I seriously *was* cheating less and less. Most of my outside communication was due to this hunt for a ménages partner, so FoXXXy and Tracy were the only online chicks still lingering around. And Tracy being so far away made it much more manageable to keep Shay in the dark about it all.

But nevertheless, it still a challenge. Shay was around me ninety percent of the time she spent in KC. And now that my sister was on the run and Shay was around my folks so much, we were as open as ever. So, it was super hard to play shit off like I was used to.

For one, this whole *'texting back and forth throughout the day'* thing wuttin' as common back then as it is in today's times. Before Tracy, Shay was actually the first person I'd ever texted so often. Me being locked in to my phone screen was a dead giveaway that I was talking to someone else. This was well before smartphones and all the mobile app activity that's normal routine now. I was slowly getting the hang of it but, like I said, it wuttin' a walk in the park. And Shay never made it easy with her always being up under me. Not to mention, Tracy did her own part to make it even harder, with her constant accusations that I was spending my time with someone else.

In the beginning, she made it seem like we were just casual friends and never questioned my personal love or sex life. But from the moment she went in her pockets – Tracy called herself checking me, always asking questions about who I was kicking it with. She was a nosy little something – paying close attention to any activity on my *MySpace* page and fact-checking whatever info she could find out there on me. She had somehow managed to figure out some of my basic history and info, which was crazy to me cuz I ain't realize you could find out shit about a person so easily. I guess the world was changing overnight again.

Tracy hadn't found out about Shay yet, but she was most definitely on to me. She loved to text late at night sometimes to see how fast I would respond or ask me to call her when she thought I wasn't alone.

Clever ass bitch.

The crazy thing was she didn't want that shit working both ways. For all the mystery and things I wuttin' sure about surrounding Tracy...she wouldn't let me accuse her of lying about *her* situation or hiding shit. She was quick to point out that we weren't together if I ever asked her some of the same shit she'd ask me. She would then always follow-up with how she wuttin' seeing nobody and how she ain't have time to be in nobody's relationship. Tracy loved making me think that I was the only nigga she was dealing with – but I had learned enough from **The Art of Cheating** that I knew better.

In the back of my mind, Tracy *had* to be in a full blown relationship back in Ohio. Right? At this point, I was almost convinced she was married and just looking for some attention on the side. That would explain why she was always unavailable or *'out of town'*, hitting me up from random numbers to be sneaky.

And even though *Henrietta the maid* was a real voice on the other end of the phone, it couldn't be that hard to find somebody to pose as a housekeeper for the right price. I just couldn't figure out why she would go through all this trouble just to creep around with a nigga like *me* from outta state.

Especially with the way she was breaking *bread* on a nigga.

Tracy was something like my sugar-mama now and she was sending shit without me asking. It was like she wanted to spoil me just because – trying her best to show me what it was like to fukc with a woman where money was no object. She paid my *Sprint* bill three months in full back in November, after I snapped out and told her *'don't worry about who all I'm texting on my phone when you don't hear from me. I pay this bill.'*

You know the rule where a muhfukca can't tell you who to talk to if they not paying your phone bill? Yeah. Well, a week later I found out my bill was paid up for the next three billing cycles and she hadn't even said shit to me about it.

How the fukc did she even get my billing info to do that shit??

That shit fukced me up. And not just because she paid the bill like that. I mean, it was just the *way* she did it. Her whole style felt like she was standing in front of me with a big wad of cash, throwing it against my forehead whenever I talked too crazy to her. You know – kind of like how a paid ass **trick** does a **whore** who thinks they're broke.

Shit, now that I'm thinking about it – it could also be compared to how a **pimp** reminds his **whore** that she'll never go too far without him! And in either scenario, the shit made *me* feel like the **whore** who was enticed by the **money**. That shit was eating me alive!

My niggaz would prolly think I'm on some real life **cyber pimpin'** if they knew the half, but deep down, *I* felt like the one being controlled. The money was the perfect bait for me at this point. And with my mentality putting *money over bitchez and niggaz* – I could really care less what others would think. The whole ordeal was fukcin' me up, but in the end I felt like I was doing what I had to do.

She was paying the balance on Ronnie's legal fees, putting money towards my music project, and keeping me laced with drip. I *had* to keep Tracy close. I'd be a fool not to.

So there I was, a week before my birthday, lying to my girl about where I was headed. *Again.*

Sashé was at my spot in *Overland Park* waiting on me

to *'finish mixing a track down at Jaz's'*. But the truth was…I hadn't been to the studio today *at all*. Instead, I was actually headed down to my aunt's to pick up a package delivered for me earlier that afternoon.

I had no idea what it was or that it was even coming, but I knew it was from Tracy. When my cousin called me and told me it was delivered – at first I couldn't figure out where Tracy got my aunt's address. Then I realized that it was the same address I had her using for those *Money Grams*, and what a mistake that was.

Man, so she's bold enough to start actually mailing shit now, nigga?

Yeah, that coulda been a real disaster if Shay happened to be around to intercept that package, bruh.

Facts, and that's all I was saying. We gotta tighten this shit up before it gets any further outta hand, dawg.

As I made a left off the highway onto *Van Brunt*, I started thinking to myself how lucky I was that my half-Mexican cousin, **Saleena**, was the one who signed for the package. Had it been *anybody* else...I might be in for some heavy damage control.

Saleena was one of my favorite older cousins and first teachers in **The Art**. She gave me so much game at an early age about how to play my cards that it made me determined to do the same for her only son, **Lil Rico**, as *he* grew from a boy to a man. Saleena couldn't give her son the game the way she gave it to me; she'd always look at him like her baby, as any mother would.

Lil Rico ain't know his mama the way I always had, and I understood what my role was between the three of us. But I also understood how *protective* Saleena was of her son. She *still* ain't know shit about Lil Rico's drunken night at my spot with Sashé and friends last summer. And I planned on keeping it that way for a long time – maybe forever.

My big cousin was standing in the doorway with the box in hand, cheesing with that mischievous grin as I walked up the steps. I shook my head as her as I opened the screen door, "Whaaat? Yo ass!"

"Uhn uhn!" she stopped me. "Nah, nigga – *yo* ass!!"

"Man, what you talking about, cuzz? I ain't did shit. I been good."

"Yeah, right," Saleena wuttin' having it. "Who is this from, Little Rodney???"

Man, I hate when she call me that!

Nigga, seriously I hate when anyone call you that stupid ass shit! Gotdamn, yo!!!

"Shit, I don't know," I glanced down at her hand. "Lemme see it."

Saleena jerked away from me and moved towards the middle of the living room as I reached for the small package. The box was about the size of a small speaker and didn't appear to be heavy.

"Yeah right, *you don't know'!!* It's from somebody in *Ohio*. Who you know in Ohio, Rod?"

"Nobody," I lied with a straight face.

"Yeah, right!" she started yelling in a high-pitched frenzy. "Nigga, you been creeping with somebody in Ohio – I know you, boy! Now what if somebody else was here when the mail came? You slipping, Lil Rod! I know I taught you better than this."

"Man, I got this," I motioned to her hand again. "For real, lemme get it.

She finally handed me the package with a smirk on her face, shaking her head, "Mmmm hmm, okay! You gon' get caught up, nigga, out here being sloppy! And Sashé might cut you, nigga! It be them sweet ones you gotta watch out for!"

"Man, shut the hell up, girl! How I'ma get caught when I ain't doing shit??" I asked her arrogantly. "Back up off me – I'm space age!"

I took a seat on the couch to look over the package. The sender was *I. Evanston & Associates, LLP* and it was addressed to my *full* government name – even with the Jr. at the end. It didn't *appear* to be a gift from somebody I was seeing on the side – but Saleena was right. This was *sloppy as fukc.*

As my original mentor, it was more than enough for Saleena to make a big deal out of. That's how you stay on your toes in **The Art of Cheating** – the seasoned masters gotta be able to smell yo shit from around the corner. And critiquing is ever necessary.

But, at the same time, I was *also* right. I was space age with the shit I was on and had been for years. Saleena will still argue to this day that I never cheated on **KeLLy,** and *that* was solely a testament to how much I kept things under wraps. All I needed to do was find *that* HoLLyRod again – so I could figure out why Sashé had me slipping.

"Open it up, *space age!!!*" Saleena was getting impatient. "Let's see how you much you worth to this one."

"Yo nosy ass," I tore the box open and sat it on the table in front of us. There was a big envelope with a birthday card and my name on it. As I picked it up with my right hand, the rest of the package contents got revealed. I noticed a DVD copy of *Above the Rim*, one of my favorite movies. Next to the movie was a black, unmarked box – obviously a jewelry case of some sort.

Saleena went straight for the black box and skipped to the other side of the room, near the front door, "Ooooo, nigga, I'm telling!!!"

"Stop playing, cuzz," I shook my head at her threats. "Come on, lemme see what it is."

I then started opening the envelope and pulled the card free. It was a *Hallmark* **Mahogany** card that I didn't read immediately, as I spotted the $100 bills inside before I could make out the words. There were *28 bills* in all and each one had a birthday candle drawn on it. I stashed the bills quickly in my pocket as I looked up to make sure Saleena hadn't noticed me flip through them. But I had nothing to worry about. Saleena paid me no attention as she just stood there with her jaw dropped at what was in the black case.

"Little Rodney!!!"

I got up to move towards her, cheesing, "What is it? Lemme see..."

"Now I just wanna know one thing: how often are you hitting this one?"

I reached out for her arm, again unsuccessfully, "Man, whatchu talking about? Come on, quit playing, esé! What is it?"

Saleena finally handed me the black case, shaking her head, "Nigga, that's why you been outta town lately! Uhhn uhn – you putting in work on some lil girl in Ohio!"

I ignored her assumptions and looked down at the box…unsure of what to expect. The bright diamond and stainless steel **Movado** watch looked good enough to eat.

"Now how you gonna explain that Mr. Space Age??" Saleena fussed as I stared in awe.

That's what the fukc I'm talking about, nigga! Jackpot!

Bro, you gotta be fukcin' kidding me!

What's the problem, fam? You said it yourself! Good enough to fukcin' eat!!!

Yeah, nigga! But impossible to fukcin' hide! Fukc my life!!!!

Even Saleena could tell by the look on my face that I was more than worried. But I was determined to not *let her see me sweat*, grinning from ear-to-ear as I muttered nervously, "Man, chill out. *I got this.*"

*   *   *   *   *

7

I had dodged Tracy for nearly half a year to this point – constantly making up excuses to not do things exactly her way. It had become our ritual, of sorts.

The routine was consistent. She would tell me she was sending a specific amount of money at a certain time. But then she'd either not send it in full or make me wait, paying me in installments. Other times, she would ask me to meet up with her out the blue, with no planning ahead. Just stupid shit. Tracy did things on her own terms and at her own pace. Needless to say, it quickly became annoying as fukc. But by now, I knew it was control thing.

So, once I caught on to how she liked to do shit, I stated giving her a taste of her own medicine. And I was especially good at that with females. If you can get inside the head of a woman, you can always beat her to her next move.

But being that most of our communication was through text instead of physical interactions, this was much more of a task than what I was used to. Just when I thought I was gaining the upper hand in some way, she did shit like *this*.

I was staring at the sparkling watch in my hand, knowing that Saleena was right once again. It wuttin' no fukcin' way in hell I could hide *this* from Sashé.

The clothes, the shoes, the movies, the video games — hell, even the **money** *been concealable! Ain't no way we hiding this, bruh.*

Dawg, Shay be walking around so bubbly...she might not even notice, bro.

Man, women spot jewelry with dey eyes closed! Stop playing! She gon see this shit and immediately know it wuttin' no cheap gift to myself. Fukc outta here!

Bro, stop that overthinking shit, nigga!

Dawg, with how tight money been around here lately? She still asking questions about how we paying for studio time, nigga! She gon' at least wanna talk about how much this timepiece cost me! I don't know how I'm finna justify **this** *shit, bruh.*

"You can always pawn it – or sell it!" Saleena suggested casually. "That's what I would do."

"Hell nah...I ain't bout to sell this shit," I shook my head in protest. "I need a watch."

I was already putting it on my wrist and taking a picture of it with my phone. As I said before, I knew how Tracy worked now. Before she even started bitching about *'proof that I received and liked her gift'*, I was already two steps ahead.

Technically, Tracy hadn't said a word about the package coming, although I may vaguely remember her *hinting around* to it. Regardless, I knew she wanted it to be a surprise and I knew she expected to hear from me once I got it. I wuttin' 'bout to give her the satisfaction of finding something else to trip on, so I started snapping away.

Yeah, nigga — you ain't that concerned about Sashé finding out!

Dawg, cut it out! Not right now, nigga. I still gotta avoid the discussion at all costs somehow...

Man, it really shouldn't be no big hurdle anyway, nigga! The last thing Shay gon' think is that you getting gifts or money from some other bitch. Right?

See, man...you on dat bullshit!!!

Nigga, I'm tryna tell you her bubbly ass ain't gon even pay attention, nigga!!!

*Nigga, what you mean?!? Sashé once **was** that 'other bitch'! Spending money on me and buying me similar gifts!!! She ain't stupid, nigga! You know this shit ain't normal!*

Unless it is, nigga. Sholl look like it's common to me, big pimp. Let it play out...

I don't know, man. I mean, I *might* be able to keep Shay from assuming the watch is from another chick. Back when *Shay* was that other bitch, I was spending most of my time with her. And now that she's my main, I *still* spend most of my time with her. She knows that; she keeps tabs on that. If I just keep things the way they been, Shay 'a likely never assume the worst. We be with each other way too much anyway. When would I have had the time to cater to a generous sugar mama???

Ok, you right. I got this.

Cuz you know Shay don't be tripping. You can just say you got the watch off the streets and she 'a never second guess it.

Maybe I **was** *overthinking shit again. Shay trusts me. I just gotta remember that and keep my cool.*

Shit is different with Sashé, dawg.

Always has been…

I started typing a message to Tracy, falling to the couch as Saleena picked up the envelope to read my birthday card. She had the biggest smile on her face, clearly tickled at my antics.

My cousin was still beautiful in her late 30's, her long and wavy hair confirming her Hispanic roots. Saleena's dad, **Big Cortez,** was full-blood Mexican and one of the biggest players in Kansas City history. He was a true legend in **The Art of Cheating**, comparable to *Grandpa Jerry*. Saleena had more brothers and sisters out here than I could keep count of and we were always meeting another one of their siblings as the years went by.

"Boy, who you think you are?!?" she snapped me outta my thoughts.

"I told you I'm HoLLyRod!" I boasted, getting back in character. "Act like you know."

"Whatever, boy! You're *Little Rodney*."

"Aye, man! Quit calling me that!"

"Nigga, I don't care how grown these lil females think you are," she smacked her lips. "You'll always be Little Rodney to me!"

I shook my head at my cousin as I finished preparing the caption and pic to finally message Tracy.

ME: "Wow really??? I'm speechless."

Her reply came within a couple of minutes.

TRACY: "Try saying 'thank you' first. Glad u got it. It looks nice on u."

Damn, it's crazy how these texts are getting even faster. This 3G life is really the shit.

ME: "Thank u baby."

TRACY: "I'm 'baby' now? See that wasn't so hard. You're welcome. I just want you to have a happier birthday this year. And u needed a watch."

I sat there quiet for a second, looking at her message.

See, man she tryna be funny n'shit! I bet she sent this watch to send me a message, nigga.

Maaaan, what the hell you talking about now?

Nigga, I know you remember we got in a argument last month about me losing track of time!

Ok...and, nigga?

You don't find it ironic that she telling me how I 'needed a watch'? Come on, cuzz...

The silence in the room was suddenly broken as Saleena started shouted loudly, "Oooo, hold on! What's this, Lil Rod???" She was clearly excited about something else in the box on the table.

I only looked up for a second as I received another message from Tracy.

TRACY: "I want u to use some of the money I sent for Ronnie's invoice, and then some to get your outfits for the weekend. Are u gonna be able to come or will a stand me up again??"

Wait, what? Come where? Outfits? For what weekend??

Saleena obviously knew more than I did. As I read the text from Tracy in confusion, my cousin was asking damn near the same question, "Wait! Sooo, you going to Vegas too, nigga??? Is this a real plane ticket, Rod?? Are you serious?!?!"

Wait! **WHAT??**

"Hold on, what you talmbout, cuzz? What you looking at??" I stood up next to her to read the ticket she was holding in hand. Sure enough, it was a *one-way flight* to **Las Vegas, NV**, departing **February 16th**. Three weeks from *today*.

Saleena was jumping up and down with excitement, "Oh, Little Rodney! What the hell type of stuff you been on??? Lemme find out you out here being a *gigolo!!!*"

"Man, wait a minute, man. I don't know what this is about, for real," I insisted, truthfully speaking.

Saleena just laughed hysterically, "Yeah, okay! *Whatever,* nigga!"

I couldn't do nothing but stand there with a puzzled look on my face, mouth open and tongue in between my teeth. I really wuttin' expecting none of this madness. I felt blindsided from every angle.

Dawg, this shit crazy as fukc.

Nigga, how did you not see this plane ticket in the box anyway???

Fukc that! Why the fukc would she just plan a trip to Vegas without fukcin' saying something to me about it first?!?

Let it play out, nigga...

See, dis dat bullshit I be talking about! That prima donna shit!

Man, just holla at her, nigga. I don't know why you even tripping...

Cuz I know as soon as I say something to her about it, she gon be on some other shit! She ain't gon' see shit wrong with this, like always.

She wants what she wants when she wants it.

That's the fukcin' problem, nigga!

ME: "Uhm. Sooooo...how the hell is this supposed to work??? Why wouldn't you tell me about this trip u planning???"

TRACY: "Oh here u go..."

ME: "Seriously! Why do u do shit like this???! I told u we gotta plan this type of shit ahead!!"

TRACY: "But that's in 3 weeks Rodney! This

is what planning ahead looks like. Start clearing your schedule, it's not that hard. Stop acting like that."

ME: "See there u go with that 'clear ya schedule' bullshit! You know my situation!"

TRACY: "You damn right I know your situation. And u promised me last time."

ME: "Maaaaan...for real?? Vegas?? What are we supposed to do in Vegas?!?"

Man, fukc nah, man. I only been to Las Vegas one other time in life and ain't thought about going back.

That was before me, though, Rod!!

Yeah and that's the point, nigga. I know what you thinking. Another trip to Vegas could be life-altering. Nah, man.

You always thinking the worst, nigga!

And you always doing the most, nigga! Just like Tracy! What the hell is this bitch planning for us this time???

TRACY: "We're going to celebrate your b-day. And you said you've never been to a NBA game. So you have to go baby. Let me do this for you!!!"

Man, Las Vegas don't even have no NBA team, bro! What the fukc is she talking about?!?!

ME: "Vegas don't have a damn NBA team Tracy! Dude you are fukcin' tripping!!!"

I stood up to walk towards the door, mumbling under my breath, "This girl is so stupid!!"

Saleena was having a field day at my expense, "Oh, what? You texting her now, huh? Yeah! Get ya hoes in check, partner!!!"

"Shut *up!!!*" I barked in frustration, both at my cousin and the situation in general. To make matters worse, it was cold as fukc outside, causing me to turn back around almost as soon as I walked outside. Tracy gets my blood boiling with these stunts and now I've developed this pacing shit as I text when I'm worked up. My heart was thumping.

TRACY: "Duh! That's NBA All-star Weekend."

I suddenly stopped dead in my tracks in the doorway.

Nigga! NBA All-Star Weekend...in Vegas!

Oh shit. That's right!!! Whoa…

I told you, nigga! Let it play out!!!

ME: "Oh damn, that is that weekend."

Dawg, how could I forget that shit???

Man, come on, Rod. You know we gotta go…

Bruh, but how I'm supposed to pull this shit off with Shay?!?

Saleena was now standing in front of the fireplace to my left, still enjoying every moment of my obvious despair. As if she could read my mind, she then goes, "Nigga, I just wanna know how you been screwing this girl when you always caked up somewhere with Shay!"

She get on my nerves, I swear.

"Who said I been screwing her, though???"

"Boy, please! You act just like yo Daddy! When are you gon' change and settle down, Lil Rod??"

"When are *you* gonna change and settle down???" I shot back sarcastically.

"Stay out my bidness! This ain't about me, papi," she stood her ground. "Don't try to turn this around! Maybe it's time for you to start having some kids, become a family man."

I just shook my head at her as I received Tracy's next message.

TRACY: "Make it happen Mr. Henderson. I'm walking in to a mtg with the builders for the center, so don't think I'm ignoring u. Talk to u later."

ME: "Well wait hold on, how long is the meeting?"

I was still pacing around my aunt's living room frantically until I read her last text, which put me at a standstill. Now I knew it was gon' be a minute before I heard from her ass again. That's how Tracy operated. She was always on the go and sometimes couldn't finish our text convos. I still wuttin' convinced she ain't on no sneaky shit herself. Tracy could very well be more of a master in **The Art** than I am.

She would never admit it, and there was no way I could prove it – but she definitely had some shit going on that she wuttin' all the way open about. So far, I had at least found out about this guy named **Larry** that she was spending a lot of time with. She still stood on the fact that she was single...but I knew she had *something* poppin' off with this *Larry* character.

She had been on a few trips outta town with this

nigga and would text me from random numbers sometimes when he was near. In my mind, Larry was prolly her *husband*. And when Tracy abruptly cut conversations short like this, it always reminded me of how *I* was when it came to my girl at home.

Sure, she *claimed* that she getting ready to meet with the construction crew on the community center she was all of a sudden *'building from the ground up*. But man, stop the muhfukcin' madness! This might be new territory but I was nowhere new to this shit. Tracy ain't know who she was fukcin' with.

Or shit, maybe she do, nigga. Maybe she more on to me than I think…

I had painted Sashé out of the picture as far as Tracy knew; sticking to the story that I, myself, was single. I mean, I had to keep the truth about my situation from her bipolar ass. I peeped a long time ago how Tracy copped an attitude at the very notion of me being involved with somebody.

So, I decided it was best if I never revealed the truth about my relationship status. I guess I was feeling some type of way about how Tracy and I started off as just text buddies. Now she wanna claim some type of ownership on who I'm laid up with just cuz she kicking me down with cash??? I hate a possessive bitch.

Then again, maybe Tracy wuttin' possessive at all. Maybe she already *knew* the truth and gave me such a hard time because she just wanted me to own up to it.

But why would she keep sending us shit like this if that was the case???

I don't know, man. None of the shit was adding up. Sitting there on my Aunt Betty's couch, trying to make sense out of it was mind boggling to say the least. But little did I realize that the *real* mind fukcs hadn't even *started* yet with Tracy. I would soon find out that this was all just a setup for the bafoolery to come.

The real test would come the week of the Vegas trip...

* * * * *

September 2007

"So what'd you end up doing for ya birthday, nigga?" Krush Groove interrupted.

It was **6:30pm** now. Any plans I had on going to the barber shop were ova wit at this point. Jaz was walking back into the control room after a quick piss break and Krush was standing in the hallway, posted in front of the doorway. His eyes were low as fukc and bloodshot red, courtesy of my good green goblin. I was sipping another cup of *Henn* and *Coke*…my eyes sitting even lower behind my *HoLLyShades*.

That was why I wore my shades at all times out in public – to hide what was happening with my eyes. You can read a muhfukca like a book sometimes, simply by looking them in the eye.

"What, nigga? How we get on my birthday now?" I

squinted at Krush. "I was just talking 'bout them Vegas tix!"

"I know, nigga!" he confirmed. "But you said she sent you all'at shit like a week before yo birthday n'shit! I'm tryna hear the story about the birthday orgy I know you had, nigga!"

"Oh, here you go!" I threw my head back, smirking. "You, too now, nigga?!?!"

"Damn, nigga what *did* we end up doing for yo birthday this year, cuzz?" Jaz started wondering.

My birthday was usually a big deal in **HoLLyWorld** – and considering the fact I *partied like Lil Penny*, it was always by design. Jaz had helped me celebrate more than a few born-days and usually ended up more drunk and belligerent than myself. The two of us could turn any party into a classic...that much was a given.

I snickered as I took another sip from my cup, "Damn, nigga, you don't remember us all going to *First Fridays*, bro?"

"*First Fridays??*" Jaz looked confused, trying to recall his drunken memory. "Nah, bro, we ain't do shit on yo birthday this year. You tripping!"

"Nah, nigga – *you* tripping! They had *First Fridays* up by the stadium! That night them bitchez had me hemmed up in the corner at the end..."

"Oh, that's riiight!" it suddenly hit him. "I met you up there with *Tre* and *Lonnie* and 'nem niggaz! I don't know why I keep thinking about last year – that was the year *before* when you ain't get out huh?"

"Yup," I nodded. "Last year I was locked in a room,

mad about my engine dying."

"Yup, I remember now, nigga! That muhfukcin' lemon!!" Jaz shook his head, thinking about my car troubles. "Damn, nigga…that was the first year we ain't kick it on ya birthday, dawg!!"

"Aww shit, nigga, you bought a lemon?!" Krush asked with hood empathy. "I did that shit, too last year. I know you was sick, nigga!!"

"Nigga, toooo sick!!" I shuddered at the thought.

I still get fukced up when I think about how **Keisha** died on me weeks after I bought her and how Shay loaned me the money for a new engine. With all the problems I'm still having with that damn car, it's hard not to think about it.

Man, lemme knock on some wood, nigga.

Yeah, fool! Don't jinx us — Keisha been acting right lately!

"Aye, but we got it in at *First Fridays*, though, boa!!!" Jaz reminisced as it all came back to him.

"Nigga, I know y'all did!" Krush exclaimed. "Wassup with the birthday orgy, though, nigga?!?"

"Nigga, what's up with some *food*, nigga?? Y'all niggaz ain't hungry?!" I suddenly felt my stomach rumbling.

"Shit, nigga…I'm starving," Krush felt where I was coming from.

"Man, y'all niggaz just *high*, nigga!" Jaz teased. "Ole munchies ass niggaz!"

"Nah, for real, bro," I was getting antsy. "Niggaz ain't ate, man."

"Hell yeah...what y'all tryna get?" Krush stretched his arms out.

"Nigga, wassup with some *Town Topic*, nigga??"

"Oh, hell yeah!" Jaz's face lit up. "That shit sound fire right now!!!"

Town Topic had some of the best burgers in Kansas City, especially when you buzzed and feeling good. The best part about that suggestion was that there was a *Town Topic* just around the corner from **64111 Studio**. We all instantly knew that was the next move without giving it another moment's thought.

"Look the number up and call that shit in, I'll run and pick it up real quick," Krush offered anxiously.

"Bet that. I'm with it."

"What y'all niggaz getting??" Jaz sat back in his chair, plotting.

"Shit, I don't know," I admitted. "I wish niggaz could just pull the menu up."

"Yeah, nigga that would be dope if we could just pull that shit up online!" Jaz started daydreaming.

"*Town Topic* ain't that advanced yet!"" Krush laughed at the crazy idea.

"Yeah, they just local." I shook my head again.

"Shit, you know it's a lot of restaurants still not fully online yet, though, nigga," Jaz reminded us of the times.

"Aww, damn – so, which one of y'all niggaz got the number?" Krush was getting impatient. "Where the *White Pages* at, nigga?"

"Nah, *Yahoo* should have the number, Jaz," I told him as he pulled up an internet browser.

"Yeah, I'm already on it."

The **Fall of 2007** was still a barbaric time in the informational age. There were no smartphones with internet-based apps in the palm of your hand, and many companies still had little to no information online. But you could at least find *certain* phone numbers with never-seen-before ease.

Some local restaurants even had their own *websites* now, but *Town Topic* was a small, family-owned spot that had been around for years doing things the old, traditional way. The bar-style diner could barely sit ten people and had a jukebox near the only entrance, making the narrow eating area a sardine-tight fit. Most people ordered to go, and it was best to call in your order so you could be in and out.

Jaz started speaking into the cordless phone handset, "Hello, yeah – I wanna place an order for pickup, please."

"I be telling these muhfukcaz at my job how hard it is to sell the land line phone cuz it's going outta style and this nigga still using a cordless phone n'shit," I pointed at Jaz, smiling at Krush.

"Aww, nigga, you know he just bought that new set!"

"Yeah, can you read the burgers on the menu real quick for me?" Jaz played us off, but I could tell he was ready to spar about his devices.

"Get the fukc outta here, bro!" I yelled at Krush Groove in disbelief. "He bought a new cordless set??"

This took Jaz over the edge, as he covered up the receiver and started shouting, "Aye, my shit got digital fax and errthang! Three handsets, nigga?!? Fukc y'all niggaz!!!" Then he paused momentarily before speaking back into the phone, "No, not you ma'am! My bad."

Krush and I burst out laughing and Jaz threw us the middle finger. My cup tipped over slightly, spilling *Hennessy* and ice on Jaz's carpet tiles. Almost immediately, Krush stopped laughing, waiting for Jaz to react. Jaz had this look of death on his face as he held the phone away from his face again so they couldn't hear.

"Aight, boa...y'all niggaz better stop playing!" Jaz was always particular about being cautious around his studio, with his expensive devices and equipment all over the place. I'd been fukcin' with him about them rules as far back as the dorm rooms...when he wouldn't allow food or drinks within ten feet of his computer desk.

My nigga.

"Aye that wuttin' me!" Krush put his hands up as a display of innocence. "That's this nigga Rod being clumsy n'shit..."

"Quit acting like a hoe, nigga," I laughed unapologetically. "I ain't even spill that much."

I walked out the control room and towards the back

of the studio, to the restroom for towels. My phone vibrated in my pocket, stopping me at the sink with another message from Shay.

SASHÉ: "So what time are you coming home?"

Dammit, man!

Her text tone ain't changed at all in the last couple of hours. She must really be upset.

Dawg, if we come to blows over this — it's gon' be our first real fight in the two years we been involved. And I still really don't know what all she's seen.

So, what we gon' do, brodie?

I need to wrap this session on up and get home to face the music. We need a plan, though, dawg…

As I circled back down the hallway, I took another look at the watch…smiling at the diamonds. Krush was in the hallway again now and caught me looking. He gave me this little grin and reached for my wrist as I got closer – checking out my timepiece, "That mug *is* nice, though, nigga."

The flossy *Movado* watch was still in sparkling good shape after these last 8 months on my wrist, catching the eyes in the room as it always had. But the real magic was in the mystery behind where it came from and I still wuttin' quite ready for Shay to find out the whole truth about my cyber sugar mama.

"Rod!" Jaz screamed from the control room. "What you want, bro??"

I texted Shay back before I answered him, though…in full-blown *'test the waters'* mode.

ME: "I'm almost done Shay boo. Why what's wrong??"

Playing dumb is always the best way to soften the blows. It usually works better when you don't try to use it on someone *who learned everything they know from you*, though. Shay texted back promptly, by the time I sat back down.

SASHÉ: "Really?? You have to ask Rodney??"

Man, I'm tired of any and everybody calling me by my fukcin' government name…

Yeah, that shit getting old…

"What's that big muhfukca called?" I yelled back at Jaz. "I need one of dem and some French toast. No pickles or onions."

I then looked down at the phone, contemplating how to respond. Without knowing what exactly she peeped...finding the right approach was a real challenge. But I at least knew that whatever Shay saw – it was in my *work phone*. Somehow, I needed to try to cover my bases from the source.

The problem was – the few chicks I had been talking to on some *'smoke buddy'* shit were all randoms and none of them had my *main* phone number. Which also meant that I ain't have access to *their* digits at the moment *either*, since everything was saved in that work phone Shay was at home looking through.

I kept trying to convince myself that if she saw messages from *them*...there was little to worry about. I could be dead wrong about that, honestly. But my gut was telling me that I needed to prepare for the worst, and Shay seeing any messages between me and *Tracy* was definitely worst case scenario.

It was starting to sink in more and more as I remembered all the details leading up to this point. Shay would be pissed if she knew what I was keeping from her.

Man, I need to text Tracy, bruh.

Maybe she was texting the work phone on accident, bro. You know how random she be...

Damn! Why you just now thinking of this, nigga?!?! That would make a whole lot of sense...with the way she was talking.

Nigga, just text Tracy from the main line and see...

Man, don't play! You know replies to Shay come first...

ME: "Look babe...Idk what u over there tripping about right now, but don't forget what we got between us. We'll talk when I get home.

I had this rule to never let frustration dictate how you replied to texts, but right now I was ignoring my principles and going the cocky route. Sometimes when you spoke to a female with enough confidence behind it, it didn't matter if you were totally in the fukcin' wrong. Having a dominant way about yourself can carry you a long way in **The Art of Cheating**. I was definitely looking for that type of swing-around with that last message.

But I didn't wait for Shay's reply. Instead, I swiftly typed out a message to **Tracy**, who I now had saved in my phone as **'TEO'** *(for Tracy Evanston – Ohio)*.

ME: "Hey did u text my other phone earlier today??"

Krush was standing next to Jaz, putting in his food order and smirking at me out the corner of his eye. That nigga still waiting to hear what else happened with Tracy, I'm already knowing. It was almost as if these niggaz forgot all about my *work phone dilemma*.

"Aight, they said it'll be ready in like twenty," Jaz told us. "Shit, I guess we can all ride down there to get it. We need some more ice anyway."

"Aye, nigga, I gotta make a move after we get this

food, dawg," I mumbled somberly.

"Quit acting like a hoe, nigga," Jaz had little sympathy for me. "You gotta finish telling this nigga about *All-Star Weekend!*"

Before I could shoot back at him, I received another incoming text:

TEO: "Oh now u decide to reply smh. I texted u from Larry's phone hrs ago. U must be with her again."

"Fukc, man! I knew it!!"

My outburst was ignored by the fellas, as Krush started walking down toward his office, still yelling down the hall at me, "Yeah, nigga – stop faking!"

"Bro! Wait 'til you hear about the NBA nigga she smashing, nigga!" Jaz relentlessly kept his foot on my neck.

"Man, there you go nigga," I shook my head at my homie's spoilers. "See, I ain't never even say all'at!"

"Yeah, nigga," he mugged me. "Whatever!"

I could hear Krush slam his office door and scurrying back down the hallway, "What, nigga?! *NBA nigga?* The Ohio bitch? Who bro?!"

"Yeah, nigga!" Jaz responded to Krush with the

swiftness as he grabbed his keys to lock up. "That one cat that play for Cleveland, nigga! Nigga, she from *Ohio*, nigga! I don't know them dudes' names! What's the nigga's name, Rod?!"

"Maaaan....you talking too much, nigga! That ain't even how it went…"

Krush started pulling a black hoodie over his head, "Who this nigga talking about, Rod??"

"Bro – the one cat who from St. Louis," Jaz answered before I could get a word in. "He play for Cleveland, I think?"

I just shook my head, looking down at my phone again as Shay had just hit me back.

SASHE: "Ok. Let me know when you have your money Mr. Henderson.'

Gotdammit man!!! Now she sounds like.....you know who...

Ok. This shit 'bout to get ugly, nigga.

I told you, bro!!!!

"Oh, nigga!" Krush yelled out suddenly. "I know who you talking about now, nigga! Ole boy – **Hughes**!! Yeah, he came outta *SLU*, fool! That's who you talking about??"

Jaz had this devilish grin on his before he started screaming hysterically, "Yeah, nigga – **Larry Hughes**, nigga! That's his name! Bro, tell this nigga what you ended up figuring out, Rod! Quit playing, nigga!!"

*   *   *   *   *

8

One thing y'all can never say is that I don't give fair warning. I mean, hell, as far back as I can remember, I always gave advance notice to a bitch on what type of situation she's getting herself into fukcin' with me.

Remember how I warned **Sassy** how addictive the sneaking around could get? How I told *Mona* the night before my **Hangover** that she was headed towards doing some shit she could never take back?

Don't forget how I gave a disclaimer that my story of **HoLLy BeLLigerence** wuttin' for the weak at heart!! Or how I tried to warn y'all about how clever and strategic I could be with **The Art of Cheating** when I was searching for answers during **KeLLy's Revenge**. Errbody should know by now how these things go in *HoLLyWorld,* with all the twists and turns I took y'all through with the **HooKup** and my journey towards **Ménages**…

Let it be known that this **Cyber Pimpin'** tale ain't been no different thus far. More times than not, I'ma try my best to give a heads up with all the shit I be on. But I swear on my life – you can't make this type of shit up...

Jaz knew the deal; there should be nothing that could really shock him at this point in my timeline. Most of my other close circle were technically in the same boat.

Ricky hadn't been around as long as Jaz but being in

the same frat meant that Rick and I ended up on similar missions – both together *and* separate. As Nupes, we shared somewhat identical experiences by default.

On the contrary, Jaz *hadn't* been around quite as long as the high school homies. **Lonnie**, **Tre**, **Steve**, and **Blayze** were all around for my early development in **The Art**, and they had episodes of their own that you couldn't pay a muhfukca to make up.

Dell and **Kam** were my *hood family*. The three of us got started out here together and these type of chronicles had been building up for years in the making. But lately, shit had been getting more and more off the chain for yours truly. I had started keeping some of these details behind most of these stories to myself, partly because shit started happening so fast. But *mostly* because niggaz couldn't help to think I was lying about some of the bizarre shit that happened.

Even I couldn't believe this shit my *gotdamn* self sometimes. And if the people who knew me *most* were non-believers at times, I knew it was only natural that a muhfukca new to the way shit flowed in *HoLLyWorld* would have the hardest time ever processing this shit.

But they can never say I ain't warn 'em ahead of time.

Krush Groove couldn't say that if his life depended on it. But even though he'd been given all the proper disclaimers and warnings that this shit was filled with classic, crazy jaw drops, I still wuttin' really planning on letting him in on the *whole* truth.

The truth about **Larry** was still up in the air at the moment and Jaz was the only person I had confided in so far. In his drunken excitement, that fact must've slipped his mind – and now *Krush* had to be let in on this shit. I'm always leery about *who-knows-what* in the dirt I'm out here doing. I learned long ago that the secret to a successful career of **cheating** is *moving in silence.*

"Aye, man," I warned Krush. "You can't say shit about this to *nobody*, dude. *For real.*"

"Nigga, I ain't gon say shit," he glanced over his shoulder from the driver's seat. "I ain't even that kind, bro."

"Nah, nigga – no bullshit!" I reiterated. "This hoe ass nigga Jaz shouldn't 'a even have brought it up, nigga!"

Jaz started screaming from the passenger seat, "Nigga, fukc – I said *my bad,* Rod! I tripped, nigga – damn!"

"I ain't tripping, nigga…I'm just saying. You know how I move, nigga," I shot back.

"Rod, bro...I ain't bout to say shit, nigga," Krush chimed in with reassurance. "You know my girl got babies by a couple of well-known rappers in the town, nigga. What I look like running my mouth about shit I heard?? Come on now."

Krush then took a right turn onto *Broadway* and headed south. *Town Topic* was just up ahead. My munchies were really kicking in now; mouth just watering thinking about that French toast.

My phone vibrated again in the palm of my hand with two new text messages, back-to-back. I looked down at the screen, sitting back against the seat. I noticed how low my battery power was and made a quick mental note to change it soon. You had to keep a spare battery pack with cell phones nowadays, with all this texting back and forth becoming the thing to do.

My new **LG** *Muziq* flip phone was real **HoLLy Digital**, too, and had only cost me a fraction of the ticket for **Apple's** new *iPhone* that dropped that summer.

Sure, the *iPhone* had the fancy touchscreen bullshit, but my lil *LG* was fully loaded. You could browse the web and play videos at lightening quick speeds – and with full access to the new *Sprint TV* service – I could even watch *MTV* on my shit. Plus, it had the *external* screen with a full color display and music control pad! I could see who was calling or texting without even flipping my phone open if I wanted to. For this text from Tracy, though, I wanted to.

TEO: "How many times do I have to say u don't have to lie? I'm not stupid Rodney."

ME: "Never mind that. What did you say in the text? I didn't get it."

TEO: "I sent you the property list."

ME: "The property list??? You sent that today??? To my other phone???"

Fukc, bro! I hope she don't mean what I think she mean, dawg.

Stay cool, Rod...

I let out a long sigh as Krush parked his Saturn. Jaz took his seatbelt off almost immediately and hopped out to go grab the food.

"Aye, grab some ketchup, nigga!" Krush reminded him.

Jaz slammed the car door, "Fukc you, nigga!"

"Damn, nigga! What I do?" Krush threw his hands in the air, turning around to face me.

"That nigga just drunk, bro. Don't pay him no mind."

"Yeah, that nigga's a hoe," he joked before going back to probing my story. "Aye, but for real, though. I ain't even that type, Rod."

I was still stating down at my phone, waiting for Tracy to text back, so I only halfway-heard Krush. He mumbled something else to me I couldn't make it out as a police car suddenly sped up *Broadway*, flying north up the hill with sirens on.

"Man, I can't stand the fukcin' police, bro!!" I shuddered.

"Damn, them niggaz dipping, too! They after somebody, nigga!"
"They always fukcin' with somebody!" I shook my head in utter disgust. "Aye, nigga – yo tags straight, right?"

"Yeah, nigga, my shit legal," Krush chuckled. "Ole paranoid ass nigga!"

"Nah bro, I just don't wanna run into no dicks, man. For real," I explained.

"Aight, I feel you. Chill out, nigga. My shit straight; we ain't getting pulled over."

I had no choice but to take his word for it. I wuttin' worried about going to jail, per se. We left the weed at the studio and my gun was registered in my name – so it wuttin' like we was riding dirty. But ever since Ronnie caught the case, the boys kept looking for any reason to catch her people up in the middle of some shit. Every officer in the town knew who my sister was, so moving with caution was forcefully crucial.

"I'm just saying, cuzz. You know how shit get around this hoe."

"Aww, you know I know, nigga. We good, real talk," Krush reassured me.

"That nigga Jaz brought his heat?" I wondered.

Krush started fumbling around under the front seat. "I don't know...I don't see that mug."

"He prolly left it at the studio, it's cool. I'm just 'noid – you right."

"Yeah, chill out, nigga! We ain't out here breaking laws, nigga!" he tried to get me to lighten up.

"I know, dog," I shook my head. "Shit just been stupid lately, bro."

Jaz was finally coming back with the food, walking out of *Town Topic* with the infamous white paper bags. Soon as he opened the car door, the heavenly aroma started making love to my nostrils...causing me to lick my lips with anxiousness.

"Yeah, I'm already knowing," Krush replied in a

relatable tone. "That nigga Jaz was saying something earlier about yo brother getting caught up. Shit's all bad."

I sat up towards the front seat, taking a sack from Jaz as he got settled and put his seat belt on. Without missing a beat, he hopped back in the conversation like he never left while Krush put the car in reverse, "Yeah, nigga that's what I was gon ask you! What they talking 'bout with that nigga Dell??"

"Man. My nigga gotta sit down for a minute," I hated to break the news.

"Damn...like *for real* sit down???" Jaz's jaw dropped.

"Nah, I mean – I think he just gotta finish his backup," I pointed out. "He might do a year and a half, if that.

"Nigga. But *still.*"

"I know nigga – I'm saying! That nigga was finally getting serious on this music shit. I'm hurting, bro."

Dealing with my sister's legal issues had already taken its toll on me as the fall season of **'07** was underway. After Ronnie went into custody in the spring, my focus and responsibilities started to shift. I'm still not if sure for the better or for worse. Bringing my circle together hadn't been easy...but like I said – it all seemed to make the most sense at the time.

My brother and sister, Dell and Ronnie, were real close. He looked after her when I left and went to college years ago…and they've been tight ever since. Ronnie was younger than us both, and always caused havoc with Dell's lil brother, **Lloyd** – even at an early age. By the time I graduated and came back home, my younger family had grown up in a major way. But for all the shit they were into out here in the streets, there was something special always brewing deep down inside the core of what made them who they were.

Dell and Ronnie had the potential to be dope ass artists on the mic. Their voice patterns and flows came so naturally. Bar after bar – these two could spit for days. To them, it was never something to be taken too seriously, though. They were recording songs in the basement or at the trap house just to pass time.

I can remember how I used to try to talk them into going to **64111 Studio** to record with Jaz to put down some real shit. But they both blew me off for years. They were modest about their talents and couldn't see any serious career in music, much like I was before recently. But after all the time I'd spent around Jaz and Ricky in college, I knew Dell and Ronnie had a shot. The whole time I was with **KeLLy**, I pushed the issue every chance I got.

The most talented in the crew was our cousin **Kam'ron**, who went by the stage name of **Filthy Fattz**. *Filth* was a little less modest in his talents and ended up recording his first official project down at **64111** before I broke things off with KeLLy a couple of years back. He took it and ran with it, moving outta town to chase a record deal. By the time Ronnie went on the run, Filth was way up north in Alaska, recording with some underground legends. I was happy as fukc for my nigga, glad he got up outta this hell hole and was making a name for himself the right way.

The punk ass authorities had my sister on the same most wanted list as vile criminals like Osama bin Laden. They relentlessly harassed my family for months before we could do anything about it, searching homes without warrants and following us around. They helped feed the crooked media all sorts of bullshit narratives and dragged my family name through the mud publicly and without any remorse. If we was gon' beat this case in court, it was gon' cost to get the upper hand. Getting lawyered up meant getting *papered* up and everybody suddenly had a role to play.

When the Feds finally rushed the apartment where Ronnie was hiding out back in April – they were so hellbent on bringing her in without violence, they just took her into custody without trashing the place completely. The homies acted fast after the boys left the scene and took all of her belongings to a safe place. Then, a week later, one of her shooters pulled up on me with a computer, telling me, *'Ronnie said I'd know what to do with what was on it'*.

To my surprise, Dell had set up a microphone in the closet and helped her record a bunch of music the whole time she was on the run. The quality of the audio was beyond horrendous, and I ain't know the first thing about how to clean it up. But I knew someone who *did*.

Jaz was a genius behind the mixing boards, and he immediately committed to sorting through the tracks with me at a discounted rate for studio hours. Even at the reduced rate, though, I really couldn't afford to put my extra bread into something like this without an immediate return. But **Tracy's** generosity had opened up new doors and created an opportunity for us to move how we wanted to move.

Jaz and I had worked on those audio files for hours upon end, piecing it together with unbelievable precision. We literally spent the whole summer trying to salvage enough of the songs to turn it into a full body of work, in hopes of finishing Ronnie's project while she impatiently awaited trial.

The direction of her mixtape was challenging to put

together without her being in the lab with us, but eventually I was able to get Dell in the studio to help fill in the blanks where needed. Once Dell got a feel for the way Jaz ran his sessions, it lit a spark in him I hadn't seen before – the spark I was waiting on all along.

But the *police* just wouldn't let us be. By the end of the summer, Dell was locked up again on a bullshit probation violation. His arrest had left me back at square one – working on this music shit *alone* again.

"We can always move the release back and wait on him to come home," Jaz suggested.

"Shit, we might have to, bro," I mumbled, looking up at the car ceiling.

"That's a little minute, though," Krush shook his head at the thought.

"Man," I sighed. "I need him to redo that one track!"

"Yeah, man. It'd be nice to get that track done, for real," Jaz agreed with me.

"But, man, I'd hate push the whole mixtape back for that, though."

"That'll give us more time to clean it up," Jaz looked for the silver lining. "Make that shit really sound dope."

"It might work out for the best, Rod," Krush chimed in. "You never know."

"Yeah, it might. I don't know, though. What am I supposed to do 'til then? Nigga, that's a long time!"

Jaz turned around to face me, "Keep working on yo

shit, nigga!"

"Yeah that's what I was gonna say, nigga! Keep building yo buzz."

I shook my head repeatedly at them, "See, man, but I ain't tryna do this music shit like that for real, though!! My role supposed to be smaller, you know the plan, nigga!"

"Nigga, quit acting like a hoe, nigga!" Jaz snapped back aggressively. "You getting the hang of that shit now, bro!"

"The shit don't sound bad, Rod. That one you did today was dope." Krush turned his blinker on as we approached *17th Street*.

"I gotta listen to it again when we get back. I need to get to the crib for real, though, cuzz."

"That's what this nigga back there tripping over, nigga!" Jaz busted me out. "Did Shay ever text you back?"

"Yeah, man. She saw some messages from Tracy – I'm pretty sure now."

"Damn, nigga," Jaz frowned, realizing shit just got real. "That's all bad."

"I know, man. Fukc, bro!"

We rode in silence for a few...the three of us letting everything sink in. I knew I had to face the music with Sashé soon. I just hated being *forced* to face the music.

The irony.

"Aight," Krush finally broke the still, chilly air. "So, what's next then, nigga?"

*   *   *   *   *

<u>*Valentine's Day 2007*</u>

She was a season ticket holder. Every home game the *Cleveland Cavaliers* had…Tracy was right there in the stands. Some of the random trips she took were to cities the *Cavs* were traveling to for a road game. At first, I was thinking she was just a dedicated fan with money. But the week of the *All-Star Game* trip revealed just how involved Tracy really was with the team.

So, I was sitting on my couch watching the *Cavs* play the *Utah Jazz*, texting back and forth with **Shay** about how neither of us considered *Valentine's Day* a real **HoLLyDay**. Well – *sort of*. Sashé was actually throwing me for a loop at the moment, telling me how she wanted to hang out officially for the holiday this year.

Now keep in mind – we done had plenty of discussion about *Valentine's Day*. And last year, in **2006**, we were both still somewhat dealing with our ex's, so we didn't really make a big deal out of it. For Shay – most of the seven years or so she was with **Keith**, they were stuck in a long distance relationship and didn't celebrate the occasion like most couples did traditionally. For myself, although KeLLy and I *did* celebrate the day a few times in our four years together, *last year* was kinda shaky for us…as I was cheating so much with Sashé that I had technically moved on from the relationship. So, once Shay and I became official last year, we both decided that we wouldn't make a big deal out of the day going forward.

Unless we DID.

SASHÉ: "Ok ok ok. I'll admit that I said I'd rather not celebrate it before. But Daddy look how far we've come since then! Don't you WANT to celebrate our love for a day?!?"

ME: "Silly me. I thought we celebrated our love everyday around here..."

SASHE: "Stop being funny! You know what I mean!"

ME: "I'm just saying! That's what YOU said, not me! I told u I was used to celebrating with KeLLy."

I looked up from my phone after sending the last message, squinting my eyes at the tv screen. The game was close in the 4th quarter and **LeBron** was struggling. I think he was actually scoreless so far. Hell, the whole *second half* had been a disaster for the King; he was getting D'd the fukc up and was clearly frustrated. Now he sat on the bench with a look of defeat on his face…and I couldn't be happier.

"They gon fukc around and lose this game," I mumbled to myself under my breath, glancing back down at my phone screen. Then I hit the **Back** button to get to my **Message Inbox**, thinking this was the perfect time to talk some shit through a text – something I had become kinda good at.

ME: "The King looking more like the prince's assistant lololol..."

I didn't expect Tracy to text back right away this time. She may not be paying her phone any attention right now as she watches her team struggling live. I wondered how close her seats were; if I could catch her in the stands on camera. She never texted back during the games, only before or after once she got back to her car. Still, I couldn't pass up the chance to get my cyber taunting on. I was sick of all the hype around *LeBron*, how the world was calling him *'King'* even though he had yet to have a *Finals* appearance. Tracy was the only *Cleveland* fan I knew – this was before all the *bandwagon fans* sprouted up all over. But she was sincere in her fandom, and I knew it was the one thing I could get under her skin about.

*"I mean, a **Cleveland** fan? Really?!?"*

"Yeah, that shit unheard of, for real, nigga."

The next text I received was from *Shay*, and I quickly hit the **Back** button a couple of times to get to the **Inbox** again.

SASHE: "So it shouldn't be a big deal if I wanna do something special this year! We can just go to dinner or something Rodney. Stop acting like that."

She gotta be serious now, calling you by ya government name like that.

Dawg, I really need to start setting the standard with how errbody addressing me these days.

Yeah, nigga — cuz when was the last time you actually called Shay by her full name?

ME: "Acting like what? You acting like you brought this up before now. You acting like TODAY isn't actually Valentine's Day Sashé."

The crowd didn't like the last call, as booing started pouring out my surround sound speakers. One of the *Jazz* had fouled the *Cavs* center, **Varejão**, sending him to the free throw line. *LeBron* was checking back in the game, his *Cavs* down by 1, with like 7 minutes left.

Dat nigga ain't bout to do shit anyway! They need to leave his bum ass on the bench!!!

SASHE: "I know it's today! Duh!! We don't have to celebrate today, I know you don't wanna drive down here so I said I'm gonna come home this weekend now. Why are you being so difficult?!?!"

Shay wuttin' budging; she was switching up on a nigga real quick. And all of this was throwing me off like hell. I just shook my head, knowing that I was gon' give in and give her whatever she wanted anyway. It wuttin' like she ever asked for much – it's just the *principle.*

Bruh, if she changing up her views on Valentine's Day…what else she gon' switch up about?

Shit, hopefully not this **ménages** *search. We getting too damn close!*

ME: "Oh hush up. You know I'm not telling you no. We don't do that around here, right?"

SASHE: "Right! So Saturday then? Can we go someplace real nice?? Like somewhere where they do valet?!?"

Valet???

Wow...ok, she really showing out now! She almost sound like Tracy, with her uppity habits!

Maybe them photo shoots and modeling checks finally going to her head...

ME: "Valet?! What are we valet parking??? Keisha???"

SASHÉ: "Yes! Don't do Keisha like that. she's been running good for almost a year!!"

ME: "Wow you're serious!"

I echoed my words audibly, screaming at the tv screen. *Utah* had hit a 3 to go up by as many, but then *Cleveland* came right back down and drove the ball to the bucket, getting the foul plus a free throw. This kid **Larry Hughes** was having one helluva game, though. I stood up in front of the screen as they displayed his stats. The nigga had 23 points and was the leading scorer for *Cleveland*.

Man, you 'a think that if LeBron struggling they wouldn't even be in this shit, but it seem like whenever he out there choking — somebody else be stepping up!!!

Nigga, Hughes is the only reason they still in the game!!!

This is that bullshit!

Shit, but that's why that brought that lil young nigga in! To play supporting role to LeBron.

Man, whatever!

Bron was still in his rookie contract at this time and *Cleveland* was paying *Hughes* big bucks. He was getting something crazy like $13 million for that season – the highest paid on the team. If only for one night, they were getting their money's worth as Hughes completed the 3-point play at the line and tied the game.

I spun back around to grab my phone off the couch, straightening up the cloth cover again. I shook my head in frustration as I headed back to my thread with Tracy.

Nigga, I'm tired of these damn covers on my couches...these muhfukcaz never stay in place! And Tracy ass still ain't texted me back!!!

Yeah, but come on now. That's expected while she at the game, brodie.

I know...you right, but damn! Aight. Lemme just calm down and keep talking my shit.

ME: "Yeah ya boy Larry bailing y'all ass out..."

Soon as I hit **Send**, the crowd went crazy again. **Deron Williams**, the point guard for *Utah*, hit a jumper on the other end, giving them the 2-point lead with 6 and a half left. *Williams* was having a good outing, too – with 30 points on the night. I'm all into the game now...

This shit just might come down to the wire – for real doe...

Sashé sends me another text, but before I exited out of Tracy's thread to read it, I stared at my last message to her. Suddenly I was caught in a trance, reading it over and over again.

ME: "Yeah ya boy Larry bailing y'all ass out..."

Wait the fukc up....

Before I could think what I was about to think, that I couldn't *believe* I hadn't thought about until *now* – the game commentators started going nuts. *Hughes* just hit *another* 3 pointer to give the *Cavs* a 1-point lead, and he now had 27 points for the game.

"Man, I know that ain't the same *'Larry'!!!!'*" I hollered. There was nobody around to hear me scream at the tv, and as I looked down at my phone at the text message...I start scratching my head in deep thought, searching for possibilities.

*Bro! What if **Tracy's** friend Larry...is **Larry Fukcin' Hughes**?!?!?!*

Nah, man! Ain't no muhfukcin' way!!!

I started immediately pacing the room as *Utah* called a timeout after getting an offensive rebound. The game then goes to a commercial break, giving me a chance to dig in.

It's been a good what – *8 months* since I been talking to Tracy now??? She always had some mystique to her in how she moved, where she got all the throwaway funds from, why she seemed so privileged. We've gotten very acquainted – about as close as we could over this time span. Until now, I just been rolling with the punches for the most part...going with my gut about some of the shit I had questions about.

But it never dawned on me before that the *Larry* she mentions so often could quite possibly be **Larry Hughes** of the *Cleveland* fukcin' *Cavaliers*.

I mean, for real, that actually makes sense! If anything it would explain why she's at so many games! Diehard fan or not – that shit cost a grip, nigga!

The bitch do just be taking random trips and spending money whenever she pleases...

And a bitch could pull that off with NBA-player type money….

Maaaan…get…the fukc…outta…here!!!

Nigga, you know I ain't lying!!!

*But see, bro — the only problem with that train of thought — this whole time we been thinking Tracy is playing the game for what it's worth! Going by the same code in **The Art of Cheating** that we live by.*

Up until this moment in time, I was starting to assume that *Tracy* was *married* to this *Larry* character. But if **this** *'Larry'* was **Larry Hughes**, then it wuttin' no way she could be married to him. Larry Hughes – if I'm not mistaken – was married to a whole *other* woman not named *Tracy*.

Nigga, she might be one of his side pieces!!

Hmm. Yeah…maybe. I just can't cross out the possibility completely that it might be him…

The Art of Cheating is real, nigga — you know that. And we all know them pro athletes got plenty of side bitchez…

*Shit! I can't argue that one. I mean, look at me — a common, hard-working man with a humble lifestyle…and **I'm** not above stepping out on **my** main chick from time to time.*

Nigga, you KNOW them niggaz with cake get it in! The Art of Cheating is universal!

Good point.

And it flows way more smoothly when you can spend more money on ya paintbrushes than most niggaz.

*Ok. But the real question is: why would she be a side piece to **that** nigga...just to turn around and make **me** a side nigga she can trick on?*

My phone vibrated again, interrupting my thoughts and turning my attention back to the game. *Hughes* was back at the line...shooting the second of two free throws. *Cleveland* was now up 85 to 84.

The vibration was a reminder from a previously received message I hadn't checked:

SASHE: "Damn right I'm serious. I'm not your side bitch anymore! Get it together mister!"

Damn, more crazy irony.

She right, though, nigga. And home comes first.

ME: "I know babe. Whatever you wanna do. I'm wit it. You know that."

Dawg, if we really knew all the details...this Tracy situation could be lifechanging. Don't front.

I mean, yeah, nigga. The shit might be major if she stop being so damn secretive, nigga!

Definitely! She prolly 'a finance the whole company, nigga! I'm telling you!!!

Sashé interrupts my plotting again with a quick response. It's like she's right there to stop my mischief.

SASHÉ: "Good. Well I want u to plan it all out so pick somewhere nice for us to go on Saturday."

ME. "Ok."

SASHÉ: "Well ok Daddy. I know you're watching the game so I'll just text you later. Happy Valentine's Day! See you Saturday love."

I tossed the phone to the couch and got back focused on the game, trying to get a grip on shit. *Hughes* was back at the free throw line and had scored the last *10 points* for *Cleveland*. With a chance to tie the game up 89-all – he then stepped to the line with confidence and knocked the two shots down with ease.

This nigga got 33 points now, yo!! This shit is crazy...

Suddenly so much more made sense now. Tracy grew up right outside of *Cleveland* and had been in *Ohio* her whole life. She was definitely a real fan of the *Cavs*; she called them all by first name as if she knew 'em personally. Perhaps she actually *did* this whole fukcin' time.

Man, why the hell couldn't I connect all this before?!?!

Nigga, that's what I'm saying! I mean, she took damn near a week and a half off to make this Cavs game in Utah today! Then she flying to LA tomorrow before we supposed to meet in Vegas this weekend for the All Star game, nigga.

This weekend?!?! The Vegas trip???

Yea, nigga! As in — two days from now...

Fukc, bro!!! I forgot that damn quick!

It slipped my mind that the whole reason I started texting Shay earlier was simply to confirm with her that I wouldn't see her this weekend! I wanted to make sure she was still planning on meeting up with her high school friend, Kris.

It was the only way I was gon' be able to skip town to meet Tracy out in Vegas, and even *then* it was still risky. Ronnie was still on the run from the police, and my availability had to be open for that situation at all times.

But shit — now Shay is coming *home* this weekend; my dumb ass just made plans to have a Valentine's Day dinner with her Saturday. She really threw me off with all the celebration talk.

Dammit man...I did it again.

Knowing I can't text Shay and start backtracking, I sunk into the couch and started to text Tracy. The game had under 2 minutes left to go and *Cleveland* was now down 6 points, after *LeBron* just hit two free throws.

Damn they saying those are his first points of the quarter, dawg...

That shit crazy...

ME: "Aye what time are you flying in to Vegas again Friday? Text me after you leave the game."

It was getting late, close to **10:30pm** now. I sat there on the couch staring blankly at the tv, eyes sitting low as fuck. But I needed them *lower*. Smoke soon filled the room from my swift spark up as I watched the last few seconds of the game.

Utah was up by 4 with 30 seconds left. Then the hoe ass European forward, **Pavlović,** hits a 3-pointer for *Cleveland* with 28 fukcin' seconds on the clock!!! It's a 1-point fukcin' game now!!!

"These punk muthafukcaz act like they wanna just lay down for these chumps!" No sooner than I blurted that out, *Millsap* from *Utah* turns the ball over and *Pavlović* comes up with the steal with like 5 seconds left. He dribbles the ball and then outta nowhere, the Croatian guard from *Utah* steps in front of him to take the charge and they collide. To my surprise...the refs don't call a foul as *Pavlović* heaves up a final shot in desperation.

"Wow!!! Great no call!!"

LeBron, Pavlović, and the Cleveland center *Varejão* were pisssssed and complaining on the court about the foul not being called. Meanwhile, I was jumping up and down with the *Utah Jazz* as they escaped with a 1-point victory in the end. I loved seeing *LeBron* lose – it was no secret I was one of his biggest haters.

I hope he never wins a ring!

My celebration was short-lived, however. As soon as I picked up my phone to talk some more shit to Tracy...I remembered the suddenly unsettled *Vegas* matter. Tracy was expecting me to be there and right now was probably not a good time to start talking about breaking plans.

Maybe I should try to push the date back with Sashé...

Nigga, is that even an option??

Man, I don't know – it's worth a shot, though!

I still can't believe she wanna honor this stupid ass day all of a sudden anyway, bruh.

Right! That shit throwing everything off! Gotdammit Shay!!!

So, what the fukc are you gon' do, Rod?!?

I fell back onto the couch, my body pulling the covers out of place again. I then calmly lit my blunt again and began flipping through the channels on my cable box, but not really paying attention to the tv screen. After about 30 minutes or so...I finally got a text from Tracy. As expected, she wasn't in the best of moods.

TEO: "Leaving the game now. Larry is very upset. Talk to u a little later."

Without hesitation...I texted her right back:

ME: "Awww poor thing! He had a helluva game tho, right?! I'm sure you'll make him feel better..."

It was possible to read sarcasm through a text now, and I knew she wouldn't like that. I was being direct, and not beating around the bush, just like she would if *she* figured out some shit about what *I* had going on.

Her reply was lightning fast:

TEO: "Don't be an asshole."

ME: "Damn baby! Why I gotta be all'at???"

TEO: "Oh how cute. You're calling me 'baby' now. Rodney I have to go, I'll tall to u later."

ME: "Yeah I get it. What time are you flying in to Vegas tho?"

I got up to take a leak after sending that last one. I could tell I was really under her skin now...but I was only halfway enjoying it. I really needed to get this weekend settled while I was bullshitting. Once I dried my hands off at the sink, I heard my phone ringing in the living room.

Two rings later and before I could make it in time, it suddenly stopped. There was a missed call from Tracy on my external screen notifications so I flipped my phone open and hit the **TALK** button. She rarely ever did voice calls – only for something urgent.

I got several rings and then her voice mail…which was weird since she just called me not even a minute ago. So I decided to call right back.

Same thing. Four or five rings and then voice mail.

Man just go 'head and text now! Ain't no reason to keep calling, nigga...

ME: "U just called? Wassup??"

Man, what the fukc, man? I wonder what that was all about…

*   *   *   *   *

Side Chick Day 2007
12:47am

For hours and hours I wondered…cuz Tracy ain't text or call me back for that long. I ended up passing out on the couch in my routine kush coma and it wuttin' 'til I woke up in the middle of the night with a crook in my neck that I finally heard back from her again.

Three **texts:**

TEO: "Rodney don't text back. Larry saw your messages about Vegas and said something to my Dad about it. Not good."

Wait. What?!?

TEO: "I've been arguing with my father about you for the last 2 hours. He looked up your sister's information. He's so mad at me."

Maaaan...what the hell is she talking about now?!?

My sister?! What the fukc man?!?!

TEO: "He's threatening to cut me off & he doesn't want me to have anything to do with you. He can't do this! Don't text back, just wait until I contact you, ok?? I'll handle my father."

All the lights were still on in my apartment as I sat there on the couch, wiping away the slobber on the right side of my face. I still was half-sleep, but fully conscious and aware of how these texts were reading.

The *one* question I needed an answer to had my undivided attention now....

Bro. Who the fukc is her **father?!???**

*   *   *   *   *

9

<u>*Side Chick Day 2007*</u>
1:48am

Valentine's Day is not a **HoLLyDay**. Some days it all just seems to go in my favor. Those days when shit just seems to fall right in my lap – we call those days the *HoLLyDays*. Valentine's Day is rarely such a day. This made-up, superficial ass holiday to celebrate love and happiness is in honor of the exact opposite of what this *Art of Cheating* represents.

V-Day represents companionship, fidelity, and romance; it's that day when you get showered with sheer appreciation from the one you adore. . But one thing it ain't…is a *HoLLyDay*. February 14th is the one day of the year when no one should second-guess their worth or feel lonely later on that night.

We all know there's plenty of long-time Valentine's Day traditions – the flowers, the candy, the surprise gifts. But one of the most universal customs is how you *end the night*. If you're lucky and everything is perfect, you hope to end up in a wet pool of love's juices…worn out from countless orgasms.

But we also know life ain't perfect and errbody can't all get lucky at the same time either. So, even though it wuttin' a *HoLLyDay* – by this horny time of night it wasn't

169

unusual for me to get some late night action offers. With the era of drunk texts moving at a lightening quick pace – if you were *HoLLy Digital* like myself, getting a random picture attached to a late night text like the following one wuttin' out of the ordinary:

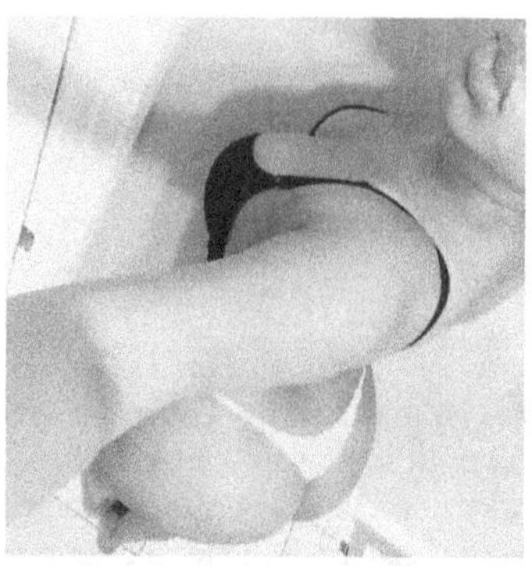

MELISSA: "For your eyes only! Goodnight stranger "

The late night alley-oop was from my co-worker, **Melissa** – this nice and thick, brown-skinned tender with a slight crush on yours truly. Now before y'all even let your dirty little minds go there – I hadn't banged this chick yet.

We'd been working together for a couple of years but remember – I was trying to do *right* these days. *Melissa* and I hung out a couple of times last summer before my sister went on the run, before shit got really real with Shay. I had since toned it all the way down with the co-worker flings, but Melissa had been throwing me flirtatious signals ever since we worked in the same department.

I played that role like I wuttin' tryna fukc for as long as I could, but the last time we were in a room alone, she just came out with it and questioned my motives. Standing there half naked after a swimming party, the words – *"Why haven't you tried to fukc me yet, Rodney???"* fell out her mouth, to my complete surprise. I didn't think she was that kind of girl and so I froze up and we never mentioned it again.

Melissa was very professional and about her business at work – but on the under she had a sexual mind that she longed to express at the right moments. This late end to Valentine's night was obviously another one of those right moments; the pussy was clearly being thrown at me yet again.

Her timing was all bad, though. I barely even looked at the picture mail, still locked in on texting Tracy.

We had been going back and forth for about 45 minutes or so now and as late as it was, I was feeling a lot of things…but tired or horny wuttin' one of 'em.

ME: "WTF man?!?! Why are u just now telling me all of this?!?!"

I could barely think straight. My vision almost felt blurred...but I wuttin' that drunk. I was both mad and scared, heart racing with adrenaline as I re-read Tracy's messages. I couldn't believe what I was seeing; couldn't figure out why I hadn't been made aware of all this shit before.

TEO: "Calm down, it's going to be OK. You just have to trust me."

ME: "Man fukc that! What u mean 'calm down??? You telling me your dad works for the fukcin' district attorney's office!!!"

Shit had really hit the fan. All of the mystery surrounding Tracy was finally starting to be revealed for what it was truly worth. I was pacing around my quiet apartment with anxiousness, letting it all sink in.

The Vegas trip was *out* – she'd decided that meeting up now was just *too risky*. I had so many *questions*...so many new reservations about this situation now. I was already thinking that perhaps I had bitten off more than I could chew again. But *now*, after all of these new details coming out, I was more remorseful than ever that I put myself in such a position.

Man, I swear you can't make this shit up, dawg...

And somehow...someway...the shit always plays out like a movie, nigga...

So apparently, Tracy was the daughter of a prosecuting attorney for the *Cuyahoga County* district in *Cleveland, Ohio*. Let's call dad **Thomas Evanston**.

Mr. Evanston was head of the largest division in the County Prosecutor's office – the *Criminal Division*. He led the team that wrote search warrants and presented cases directly to the Grand Jury – you know – the *heavy* shit. Mr. Evanston *also* had a reputation for being zero-tolerant, seeking the harshest of sentences in the court room. From the way Tracy was talking, this muhfukca was all straight and narrow and didn't take kindly to anything or anyone affiliated with the opposite side of the law – *period.*

My heart was racing even faster as I tried to remember all the shit Tracy had learned about me and my background…all the shit I'd revealed to her about my family's lifestyle. And I always knew there had to be a *reason* Tracy was so secretive. Now it made a little more sense. Her daddy didn't want his baby girl associated with the likes of me or mine and now that he caught wind of what was going on, he was ready to drop the gavel himself.

I was freaking out, starting to break a sweat in my ever toasty living room. Tracy's calm demeanor through her texts wasn't helping:

TEO: "I didn't think u needed to know all of that. Just like all the stuff you don't tell me about Mr. Henderson. Don't go there. You promised."

This bitch was really testing my patience. But she was right. There was plenty of shit on my end that I conveniently left out…shit that I always wondered if she *somehow* knew anyway. All them sarcastic hints and smart remarks she loved to throw at me had me now thinking it wasn't just all assumptions. There was no telling what all Tracy really had access to or what kind of resources she coulda been using all along to get info on me.

Dammit! I fukced up!

But you gotta play it cool now, roll with the punches.

Right…right. Never let 'em see you sweat…

ME: "Whatever. You stay on some bullshit dude! I swear!"

TEO: "I'm not your dude Rodney. I told you about that."

Just take deep breaths, Rod. Don't snap…

ME: "Quit calling me by my fuccin' gov name!"

TEO: "That's your name Rodney! What else am I supposed to call you?"

I started typing so fast with my response that I fumbled my phone in my hand, nearly dropping it to the floor. I took that as a sign to erase my initial, disrespectful reply and started over:

ME: "Man I don't know who fuccin' watching this shit! For real Tracy, calm that shit down."

TEO: "Oh please! Stop acting paranoid Rodney. No one is watching this."

ME: "How do I know that?! Why can't you just respect how the fukc I feel about it?"

TEO: "Because you're overreacting. And stop cursing at me. You promised not to snap."

Just count down from 5, Rod.

5...4...3...2...man, fukc this shit!!!

ME: "Man whatever! Fucc you."

TEO: "Wow really?? This is really how you're talking to me right now? After all the shit I've done???"

ME: "Oh look who's cussing now tho?? Fucc that! You lied to me!"

TEO: "How the hell did I lie to you Rodney? You've nvr asked me about my father! You barely ask me about anything besides money."

I was starting to get antsy as the texts kept flowing and I knew I wasn't gonna be able to keep my cool much longer. I had promised Tracy that I wouldn't blow up before she told me who her dad was, and even when I agreed to it, I already knew I wuttin' gon' honor the deal.

Anytime a muhfukca makes you promise not to snap out – it's because deep down, they know beyond a shadow of a muthafukcin' doubt you're gonna snap the fukc out once they tell you what's really up. Thinking back on it, I was surely more mad at myself than anything...but this bitch's texting flow had me boiling with bloodshot red eyes.

I hated that inkling of a feeling that she was holding shit over my head. I bit my lip, typing with more and more fury, and less and less patience:

ME: "Man fukc your money Tracy. I don't need that shit! Fucc u!!!"

TEO: "Fukc me?? You're just saying that.

You don't mean it."

ME: "Yea the fucc I do, Idgaf bout that shit fa real!! It's a trick to it apparently. Idk what type of games you been playing, but I ain't got time for this shit."

TEO: "I'm not playing games with u Rodney. This isn't a trick, I promise. I'm being totally upfront with you now."

ME: "Bitch you got dicks in Ohio pulling up my sister's name like we ain't under enough heat! Fucc your promises! For real! That promise shit don't mean shit!"

TEO: "Wait a minute...'bitch'?"

I knew that would get her attention and didn't think about erasing it this time. Fukc it.

ME: "You read it right."

TEO: "Ok, I will act like I didn't. You're tripping. My dad is concerned about ME, not you. Not Ronnie. You need to trust me. You need to calm down."

ME: "Dude you already said he don't want you having nothing to do with me! Ain't no telling what all you told him! Ain't no telling what all he know. 'Trust you' my ass!!!"

TEO: "You're tripping. It's late and you get grumpy when it's late. Are you hungry? Or horny?"

I immediately felt the instant flow of blood rushing down into the base of my dick, working against me again in my moment of fury.

ME: "Man shut the fucc up!!! You don't know me! You don't know shit. I know your dads type, how he looks at things."

TEO: "I told you I'll handle him. All I'm asking is that u let me deal with it."

ME: "You already said he called me a thug! Me?!? A thug???! Nah you on some BS, I don't fucc with u type of people."

I was fed the fukc up with folks labeling me because

of who my sister was. Even more tired of all the fukcers who were judging Ronnie from all the exaggerated news reports and police statements. This shit had seriously made life a headache for my family and I was expected to be the aspirin. This 'cop dad' situation was just gon' make matters that much worse. And since we couldn't really speak out in the media or vent our frustration until Ronnie was in custody and went to court – all of my anger had me ready to explode on somebody. *Anybody*. Tracy was an easy target on this late night, and now I was charged up enough to finally stop holding back.

This bitch got me fukced up...

TEO: "I can't believe you're talking to me like this Rodney."

ME: "Bitch stop calling me Rodney."

TEO: "Quit calling me out my name!!"

ME: "Bitch quit calling me out mine."

TEO: "But that's your name Rodney."

ME: "Well bitch that's yours."

TEO: "Smh. Why are u acting like this? Seriously?"

ME: "Whatever. Stop calling me my government."

TEO: "So what am I supposed to call you?"

ME: "I don't know. Call me HoLLyRod."

TEO: "Yeah right. I'm not calling u that."

ME: "Well bitch I'm calling u bitch from now on bitch."

TEO: "Whatever: You must be high."
ME: "Bitch I'm always high. Tell ya daddy that."

I'm feeling myself now. The more we went back and forth…the more the gloves came off. No more sugarcoating. This was my perfect opportunity to show her some classic **HoLLy BeLLigerence** with no apologies.

TEO: "Really Rodney?? You're just gonna be an asshole and talk to me like I mean nothing to you now? Over this?? Maybe my father was right about you."

I'm typing so fast now, I'm missing letters...

ME: "Fuc yo and ya daddy! An fucc Larry Huges scrubby ass too! Matter fact...fcc the entire Clevelad Cavliers! Especialy LeBron! Fucc the whole state of Ohio & evrybody n it!!"

What happened next was strange. I received another message from Tracy not even a full second after hitting the **Send** button:

TEO: "Ok I didn't mean that, I take that back. Do the same for me please..."

Damn, nigga — that was quick.

Right! She musta sent this msg before she read my 'Fukc You List'. Right?

Shit...I don't know, dawg. Unless she DIDN'T...

So now, I'm staring at her reply and this awkward

moment of silence starts to take hold. Crazy – considering the fact that I was actually *alone* and the room had been silent for hours anyway now. Still, as I'm biting my lip and lying motionless on the couch, there's now this undeniably thick aura of awkwardness in the air. Unsure of whether she's read my last message and how she's really gonna react to it, I got up and started pacing the room again.

Lemme just keep my adrenaline pumping.

Five minutes go past. I'm standing in my bedroom doorway now, checking my phone anxiously. Nothing yet.

Damn…but did I really go too far?

Nah…she said that shit talkin' 'bout her daddy was right about you, Rod! She know she was wrong for that shit!

Another five minutes pass…and then another.

Shit, but man ain't no way she coulda read my message that damn fast! She done seen dat shit by now, I know she mad as a muhfukca! Fukc!

You did go kinda hard, Rod…

That's why her ass ain't texting back!!!

I'm sitting on the edge of my bed, starting to believe she ain't gon' reply. Why would she?!? The more I scanned over my last text…the more I read the whole thread, I *was* pretty harsh from the moment she told me what was up. And that was *after* she made me promise not to flip.

Man that bitch knew you was gon' would flip, nigga.

Yeah she did! When she tried to make me put it on my Mama that I 'a remain calm — see, that's when I knew it was 'bout to be some straight babybakc bullshit.

Rereading old text messages can be a trip, especially during disagreements like this. You end up sending some shit you might feel differently about later, but the thread is always there so no one forgets. You can never deny you said it because once it's sent — it's on the record.

Unless it AIN'T…

I'd been following the rules to **The Art of Cheating** with precision and protocol — deleting messages & evidence since back in the day with KeLLy. And as I think about it, Sashé knows how I move *anyway*. I doubt she would even *check* my messages, I mean, she knows I don't slip up like that, with how we used to get down. So I probably *shoulda* been keeping some of these messages between me and Tracy. There's plenty of shit she's said to me via text that I wish I could go back and read, especially right fukcin' now.

Especially since now I'm sure *she's* doing it. Since I'm now sure she's *been* doing it.

I thought Tracy might be married...painting her own portraits in **The Art**, erasing evidence on her end. But then *tonight* happened. I done went from thinking she might be **Larry Hughes'** *side piece* to finding out the bitch is the daughter of the muthafukcin' *police*. Well, I mean, he ain't the *actual* police but he's working on the wrong side of the law and my sister been all over national news and on the run going on six months now.

Fukc, bro! I wish I could just somehow remember what all we done sent this bitch!!

I knew I hadn't been too reckless. **The Art of Cheating** borrows from the criminal mindset, so I was always cautious and hesitant about what I did on phones — especially lately. The *Feds* were watching. Confirmed by inside sources before the New Year, my whole family's main lines were being monitored...so my mindfulness had been top-tier anyway.

These punk muthafukcaz were desperate to catch Ronnie, harassing with anyone with any previous ties. I told them the last time they stormed up in my apartment they were wasting their time watching her family. That was damn near the truth, too. None of the family knew where she was. I mean, even *I* didn't know where she was laying low at myself and didn't *need* to know. When we had to communicate, it was all airtight and never from any phone that could be traced back. Dell was so ahead of the game, he had the whole crew cease from even referring to her by *name* on phones…we just knew when we had to know who we were referring to.

Ok. So, whatever text conversation I had with Tracy about my sister hadn't been incriminating – *that* much I was sure of. But still – how I wished I could look it all over right now.

Waiting on Tracy to text back was killing me, too, as I envisioned her looking over everything I'd ever said, figuring out how to use my words against me. I could see it all clearly in hindsight. The way she always seemed to twist my words around, jumping to conclusions about my situation & love life; how she would find out more info about me here and there from small details I gave her. Just like on some detective shit, piecing together the puzzle. It was in her blood. It came natural for her with logical reason.

She's probably just like her daddy…forever trying to make a case.

So it's been like 20 minutes now and still nothing. I'm contemplating just texting her back, trying to see where her head is and if she's really offended by my last words. I mean, I'm still leaning towards the notion that she sent that *'didn't mean it'* text *before* she actually saw *my* belligerent one, but then again I can't be 100% sure. Maybe she's just waiting on me to take it back like she said. That's the thing with this texting shit…when people take forever to text back, you sit there pissing ya pants anticipating their reaction – nervous about which way it's gonna go during the entire delay. At some point after so long you realize they not texting back, and you start to accept defeat.

I was at that point now, finally admitting this Tracy shit was too good to be true. Deep down inside, I always knew there had to be a trick to it.

I mean — who the fukc just meets a nigga online and starts sending them money and gifts? Who in the hell falls for a guy like me off my words and digital charm, ready to be down for me from text messaging and picture mail??? Maybe this is the best time to just fall back.

There you go acting scary again, nigga! Stop overreacting! Let it play out...

Nah, man! Like — for real! This **cyber pimpin'** *can't possibly work this way, bro. It's gotta be more to it than this. We should be happy we found this out now — she had to have been sent by the police, nigga! It all makes sense now.*

Unless it DON'T!!! Think about it, Rod...

I sighed as I wrestled with my thoughts. If I was gon' be all the way real about it — Tracy and I weren't exactly *strangers* anymore. And with all the conversation we had before any physical contact, this thing *didn't* start off as the typical lust fling. Texting leaves a lot of room for easy misinterpretation, and you can't really feel emotions through the screen or read the tone of what a person is saying. But sometimes — you talk so long with a person through so many messages, it's like you're right there *with* them. You start to read into their verbiage...you can get to know a person through texting tendencies if y'all chat enough. As much as I wanted to believe she mighta been faking the whole time, there was this other sense of intuition deep in my gut that couldn't deny the sincerity in some of Tracy's words.

*Sometimes...you just...**know**...*

As twisted as it was, deep down I knew Tracy had some *integrity* to her. I knew she'd come through for me and Ronnie, even if on her own terms and at her twisted pace. I knew she really connected with me in some ways – we sent 1000s of characters to each other on average monthly. If all of this was a trick...I'd be going against my gut feeling to admit so. As twisted as it sounded, I felt like I *knew* Tracy, even finding out tonight how much I never may have known all along...

I mean…sometimes...you just…*know*...

The awkward silence was ultimately broken at *3:32am*. There I laid – across my bed on my back, legs hanging off the right side as I held my vibrating phone up above my face in the darkness.

TEO: "Take it back Rodney. I know u don't mean that. Not about me."

Staring at her words was almost like staring in her eyes. I could see her desperation, mimicking my alarmed, worrisome state. Now *she* was the one waiting on the other end, anxious for me to reply back in her favor. I *almost* immediately did, too...since I was still caught up in that feeling of losing the upper hand. A second text helped me sit up and catch myself:

TEO: "Don't be an asshole. I took back what I said. Be fair & do the same so we can get past this Rodney. I just wanna move on."

I let out a long & loud burp as I took in her words, *Hennessy* & *Pizza Hut*-scented fumes filling the air around my nostrils.

What I tell you, nigga?! You gotta start trusting ya natural instincts more...

ME: "I'll take it back if you stop bullshitting with me. You can't expect me not to be fukced up about this shit Tracy."

I typed out each letter slowly, as my vision was kinda blurry through my now dried-out contacts.

Man, I hate having to type out the punctuation marks n'shit when I text!

Yeah, nigga…they really need to come up with some type of autofill or autocorrect for this messaging shit…

*I mean, damn – it's **2007** – what the fukc???*

My attitude is so shitty right now. Tracy's reply helps me keep composure though.

TEO: "I know u are, I'm sorry. I've been wanting to talk to u about it for a long time, I just didn't know how to tell u. U know how u get…"

See – you still got the upper hand, nigga!

Ok, nigga…you right! But here this bitch go talking again like she really know me, though.

Who cares? Just let her believe that for now, nigga!

Shit…maybe I believe it right now myself…

ME: "Well tell me everything I need to know. And then some. I'm not gonna get over this shit if u just gon keep being secretive about it, for real."

TEO: "Ok. First I need u to promise I can trust u."

Is this bitch serious right now?

ME. "You can't be serious right now...

TEO: "Please Rodney. I never ask for much, u know that."

I frowned up as I started typing the next message.

ME: "Man ok just stop calling me by my government name!"

TEO: "I don't understand why u don't like the name your beautiful mother gave u. Smh."

More frowns.

ME: "I nvr said I ain't like my name. And u didn't know my mama to know that she was beautiful, Stop that shit Tracy."

TEO: "I know your mother was beautiful. I've seen pictures."

Nigga, what??? How the hell...

Dude! How the fukc this bitch done seen pictures of my Moms, nigga???

Right! What in thee entire fukc is going on?!?

ME: "Wow. Wtf smh..."

She barely gives my reply a second thought, continuing with her agenda:

TEO: "Can I trust u Rodney?"

I sat up in the bed, leaning my back against the wall where I lacked a headboard. That was a really tricky question; trust is a muthafukca. It's almost a facade of a concept when you really think about it. I mean, who do any of us really *truly* trust? Life teaches us to never trust anyone 100% so when we ask about trust, is there a universal cap percentage we're referring to? Ain't no telling how Tracy really intended this question to be taken – even in my late night drunkenness I'm still aware of that.

ME: "Can I trust YOU? That's the real question."

Sometimes the best way to read between the lines is to ask the writer to read in between lines of your *own*. This is where the texting tables can turn, where I'm in position to make a strong counter move. I keep typing:

ME: "I'm not in a position where I can play these type of games, u know this. U just put me in a fukced up space, my first instinct is to cut all contact with u."

I'm typing back-to-back-to-back messages with

renewed fury & confidence.

ME: "And why shouldn't I? How do I know this isn't all a setup?"

This time I aim to keep replying, before she even has a chance to respond.

ME: "How do I know you aren't working against us in the background - helping investigate??? How am I not supposed to think u tried to get close to me to get close to my sister?? How the fukc am I supposed to trust that everything u do isn't for some other hidden motives??? I'd be a damn fool to trust you after this Tracy."

My breathing quickened yet again and suddenly it felt really warm in the apartment. I got up to strip naked, and then headed towards my thermostat to turn the temperature down a couple of notches. By the time I got back to my room and bed, Tracy had read my messages loud and clear, and had plenty of rebuttal:

TEO: "Can u trust ME??? Ok Rodney you really have a lot of nerve."

TEO: "For the last damned time, I'm not playing games with u Rodney!!! You're not thinking clearly. You would have to be a fool to cut me off."

TEO: "And you're no fool!"

TEO: "You obvious don't know as much about police as u think u do if u think this is a setup or I'm working with my father. Or to even think my father would be involved in your sister's case."

TEO: "There's no way you can think that the police would spend thousands of dollars on you, to get to your sister. Why would I help pay for her attorney if I had hidden motives or this was a setup?"

TEO: "You're no fool Rodney. You can miss me with the bs. As much as I do for u with basically nothing in return??"

TEO: "You really have some nerve! Is this the type of reverse bullshit you're used to pulling on them worthless chicks u deal with every day? Lol u can't be serious."

Who the fukc she think she talking to???

Dawg, I hate with a passion when a bitch thinks she know

what I have going on with other females.

This bitch ain't never met nobody from Kansas City before we crossed paths! Who the fukc she think she is to know what type of chicks we used to or that we even dealing with any other chicks at all?

Right! It's crazy how she keep trying to turn this shit around, like she ain't the one being exposed here.

See?! That's what happens when you let a bitch think she know you, Rod.

My breathing sped up even more, as I started typing as fast as I could, hands shaking:

ME: "Fukc u Tracy. U have no idea what type of chicks I fukc with. Apparently I fukc with chicks with big bank who like to trick it off on a nigga they barely know. You should feel special that I'm even dealing with u in the first place. Kiss my ass!"

I stared at the message for a couple of seconds without sending, licking my lips with pride. I mean, for real, this chick really had me fukced up. And I wuttin' 'bout to let her keep trying to pull my card like this and get the upper hand. I started thinking about how as soon as I hit **Send,** I'm finna turn my phone off and call it a night. So, whatever reply she got for me after this, I ain't gon' see it 'til in the morning.

This shit ain't going nowhere anyway, bruh.

Man…and maybe I'm tripping but I coulda sworn I just heard birds chirping outside.

You think it's too late to hit Melissa back, nigga??

Shit, I don't know — what time is it? You think she still up?

I know all this back and forth and this bitch talmbout all the 'worthless chicks we deal with every day' got me in the mood to get belligerent…

With some real playboy redemption, nigga. You know how we do….

Unfortunately, though, as I was lost in my thoughts on how I'm just gon' end this text convo so abruptly — Tracy sends *another* string of texts. stopping me dead in my tracks. Consequently, now I'm staring at her messages the same way I was just staring at my *unsent* one just seconds prior.

TEO: "Rodney just listen to me ok? Don't reply. You have no reason to not trust me. I am not playing any games, I do not have time for that. I tell you like you tell me this all the time. I am serious, and you have to learn when to let that sword down. I get that you're upset. But you seriously need to trust me. I can change your situation, if you let me."

TEO: "For one time in your life, just go

against your first mind and stop thinking I'm out to get you. I don't care what my father thinks, let ME handle him. He is a hypocrite and can't control me like he wants to so bad. I have access to money he doesn't know about, I have connections he wishes I never found out about. He is stubborn and used to running things - but he wouldn't be in the position he's in today if my mother didn't help him. I hate him for forgetting that, I hate the way he abuses his power. How he tries to hide from his past."

Damn. Where is this going???

TEO: "I need to know I can trust you Rodney. I've always been open with u, I want to be more open and honest but it has to be mutual. So I'm going to ask you one more time. CAN I TRUST YOU RODNEY???"

I shook my head and erased the message I never sent, then with little hesitation – I re-typed a better reply:

ME: "You can trust me Tracy."

Her response came seconds later. I don't know if I remember her ever replying this fast, even when we first started messaging.

TEO: "Are you sure???"

ME: "Do I really give you reason not to?? Why do u keep asking that??"

TEO: "Because I'm risking a lot with how I am with u, and because I want to not worry about it. You remind me of my father, you're just as stubborn and I know you have issues trusting people to have your best interest in mind. I'm not playing games with u. I need to be able to trust you're not just taking advantage of me - and that you're not playing games with me."

Whatever control I felt like I had regained, it was all but gone now. I was now responding without much thought in this moment, almost caught in a trance by her words. And it was rare that words got the best of me and made me thirst for more.

ME: 'Tracy look at how much u know about me, how much of an issue do I really have with trust?"

TEO: "Yes, but you don't tell me everything."

ME: "Ditto."

I bit my lip as I hit **Send**, realizing a few things in a matter of milliseconds. How texting had now become my primary form of communication – not just with Tracy, but *overall*. This was probably the first real moment of truth I had in this fact, and it was my quick response and choice of words that did it. Saying *'ditto'* made me instantly think of Shay – how all the heavy texting started with *her;* how our whole relationship started with discreet messaging. Sashé would always be special in that regard and it's ironic that I was thinking about this on this early morning after Valentine's Day. The irony mostly lied in the fact that I had never used the *'ditto'* with anyone *but* Sashé and vice-versa.

TEO: "I'm trying to. But not if I can't really trust you."

ME: "Ok. You can trust me Tracy."

TEO: "You're really the only person I talk to about my personal things, regardless of what you believe. But when you act like you're just using me, it makes me hesitant to trust u. My father tells me I'm a fool for trusting u at all, and that you'll just take advantage of me in the end."

ME: "Ok, but your dad doesn't know me. You

can trust me, I don't know how else I'm
supposed to say it."

TEO: "You're right. He doesn't know you.
Not like I do. It's the situation that scares him,
it's because of his background and how he met
my mom and how she invested in him with my
grandad's money. He's always been
overprotective. It pisses me off! Like how am I
not supposed to think that that was his motive
with my mom if that's the case?"

I kept reading in silence.

TEO: "It's like he's always wanted to
control everything! My parents argued for years
about the trust fund Mom had in my name – he's
always had an issue with any account I had free
access to, or any transactions my mother did.
My whole life I've had to go behind his back to
get the things I've wanted. It's tiring Rodney!"

I thought Tracy was kind of opening up to me a bit
before now. I mean, sure, she wuttin' being upfront about
any and everything, but like she kept saying – neither was *I.*
On this early morning – as the sun was definitely coming
up now – Tracy was suddenly laying it *all* out
there…telling me all her darkest emotions that she
struggled with.

TEO: "And when Mom passed, there was this big thing about how much money she left me and how much he was going to have immediate access to. We've never fought so much, I've just been trying to do everything I can to stay sane with him. I know I'm not perfect, but this asshole has me beat by a long-shot."

TEO: "I've even wondered lately if he really loved my mother."

Damn. This is some heavy shit. I'm still shaking my head at how fast she's sending messages, as I rub my closed eyelids, fighting sleep.

ME: "Don't say that Tracy. Of course he loved your mom. He was with her 'til the end, that's more than I can say for my folks."

A minute or two passed before I got her next message:

TEO: "Rodney my mother's headstone was barely finished before he had his new little girlfriend all up in my mother's hallways! Do you know what it feels like to be forced to accept your mom's replacement?!? I hate this woman!"

ME. "Yeah. Actually I do. Not exactly in that way, but I never got along with my stepmom. I mean I don't even remember meeting her 'til my mom was sick."

TEO: "Wow, why have you never told me this? See, this is what I mean. You don't open up to me like I have with you."

ME: "I mean, it never came up. Don't beat me up about it Tracy, you've never told me about any of this shit you're saying tonight.

TEO: "I know. I'm sorry. I just get so worked up about it. I just feel like my dad has never been all the way honest with me, and he hides shit. I know he had to be involved with this hoe while my mom was still alive. I know it for a fact."

ME: "What makes you say that Tracy? And don't take that the wrong way, I'm just asking. You assume a lot of stuff that just isn't true, you do that with me."

TEO: 'It was too soon Rodney. Did I mention she worked for him? She was his fukcin' tax attorney for 7 years Rodney! I've known her since I was a kid. She moved back to Ohio 2 years before Mom got sick. That's not a coincidence."

Sheesh.

The Art of Cheating is so real...

ME: "Damn. That's crazy for real."

TEO: "I don't know, I just feel like I can't respect how he feels about what I do with my life - there's just always a double standard with him. He was dead broke and in the streets when my mom met him. How can he accuse anybody of taking advantage of me?"

ME: "I mean you're his daughter, you can't get mad at him for wanting to not see you make the same mistakes he might've made. He only wants what's best for you, I can dig that."

TEO: "No, you don't understand. With him, it's all about public image. It's all about what people think or say about you. He tries to play matchmaker with Larry and I, because of his status. It's all about his career, his reputation.

He doesn't even know me to know what's best for me."

ME: "What do you mean by that? You're his daughter Tracy. He's been in your life forever. Of course he knows you."

TEO: "You're right, I am his daughter. But even more than he or anyone realizes or will ever know."

Wait…what?

ME: "Tracy…uhm. What? What are u talking about right now? It's too early for this."

Dawg, we really been texting this bitch all night, the fukcin' sun is coming up, nigga…

TEO: "Nothing. Nvm. Look, I'll make Vegas up to u, ok? Just let me handle him, and let me do what I do with u."

ME: "Tracy no, what were you just saying?

Like what did u mean by that?"

There's just something about that last piece she said that stuck out to me; I had to keep pressing. Another couple of minutes passed, and I sat up in the bed to stretch...my neck cracking from the stiffness.

TEO: "Can I trust you Rodney?"

Oh my God – here we go again with this bullshit!!!

ME: "Omg dude!! How many times do I have to say it??! YES!!!"

TEO: 'I'm not your 'dude' Rodney."

ME: "Ok! Yes u can trust me! Is that better baby?!?"

TEO: "So I'm baby now again huh? Smh. You're so full of it, I swear."

I took a second to scratch my head before I replied.

I swear I get so fukcin' tired of the up and downs with this chick.

ME: "Ok, so you just wanna fight with me??? Look – I'm not your dad, ok??? Stop taking out the way u feel about him on me!! I'm sitting up 'til damn near 6 in the morning with you and you're still asking if u can trust me? Like come on - wtf is that about?! Damn what are we even doing here?!?"

TEO: "I just want u to be honest with me! Somebody be honest with me at least just once in this lifetime! And I get tired of u lying to me - saying what u have to just to take advantage of what I can do for u! Just don't lie to me Rodney!"

ME: "Why do you keep saying that shit?? I'm not fukcin' lying to u about anything!"

TEO: "Ok Rodney. Well then...who is SASHÉ???"

Shit, nigga!

Bro…how the fuuuuuuuukc????

Valentine's Day is definitely not a **HoLLyDay** — never has been. And now that the sun was slowly rising on what we officially call **Side Chick Day** in **The Art of Cheating**, with the way this morning was already starting off — today ain't gon be one of my best days either.

* * * * *

10

**September 2007**

Krush was in shock, yelling loudly in the studio halls, "Daaaamn, nigga! So wait, how the fukc she know about yo girl? This bitch is with the Feds for real, bro?!?"

"Bro, you never told me this part," Jaz pointed out in disbelief. "I ain't never heard these details."

"I know, man. It's a lot of bullshit – caught me off guard like a muhfukca…"

"I'm saying – so what'd you say, though?" Krush wanted to know. "Nigga, I prolly wouldn't even 'a texted back after that. Real talk."

"Man, you know this nigga live for that shit," Jaz smirked.

"Nah, man," I shook my head. "It's more like I can't get _away_ from this type of shit. It's just the life…"

"What'd you _say_, dawg?" Krush asked again, ignoring my fake modesty. "Cut the bullshit!! How'd you play that shit off, bro?"

Calmly and quietly, I looked Krush in the eyes with a blank poker face, "Nigga. I didn't…"

*　　*　　*　　*　　*

Side Chick Day 2007
_4:11am_

My eyes were hurting. My brain felt even worse. My stomach was growling and rumbling, but I doubt starving hunger had much to do with it. It was definitely more shock and anxiety than my appetite. This whole shit had taken a silly ass turn.

It was the way Tracy played her card that had me stuck in amazement. I couldn't be too mad; it was borderline brilliant with how she held on to this. So, for a few minutes all I did was just stare at the screen with appreciation.

It wuttin' no telling how long she had known about Shay, or just how _much_ detail she already had access to. I really needed to be careful about how I replied to this.

But as if she was sitting in my bedroom with me, reading my mind...Tracy somehow sensed the sting and kept pressing:

TEO: "Hello?? Cat got your tongue now? You must be with her. I mean it is Valentine's Day. "

My back was against the wall, and my phone was shaking in my hand.

ME: "It's February 15th tho."

TEO: "Cut the bullshit Rodney. Answer my question. Who is she?"

That deflection shit ain't working, bro. She ain't going for it...

No shit, nigga! That shit rarely ever works in these moments...

ME: "I mean what do u want me to say?"

TEO: "Tell me who she is."

Man, I fukcin' hate getting interrogated, bruh...

And then we don't even know what all this muthafukca even know!! This some bullshit, dawg!

ME: "I mean, she's just a girl I see often."

TEO: "Just a girl you see often huh? See Rodney, you're full of the games."

ME: "Tracy don't do this. Clearly you've done your homework and u know who she is. What is it u wanna know?"

TEO: "I want to know who she is to you. Is she the girl you wrote all the poems about?"

Man, I know she ain't talmbout that poetry you posted on MySpace, nigga!

Of course she is! But I ain't got no reason to lie about dat shit…

ME: "No. The poems weren't about anyone in particular."

TEO: "Well I know she's the one getting all of your time while I have to beg for it. So has she been around this whole time?"

I squinted at the message, reading it very closely.

Is she asking questions that she knows the answer to or is she still searching for info?

You know the rules, nigga. Never give up the details they don't already know…

In most cases, this strategy always works. But this wuttin' a normal situation for me. I was still blown away at the fact that this chick so many miles away would even know the *name* of the girl I left my ex for. Where would she even find that information *at?* Police dad or not...I just felt like I had been moving with more discretion than this.

Apparently not, nigga.

Man, shut yo ass up!

ME: "Look, we not even together officially - ok? She's the chick I've been rocking with since me and my ex broke things off. She's not getting all of my time, no one does."

TEO: "Liar."

ME: 'That's the truth Tracy. Unless you know something I don't."

TEO: "Does she live with you?"

ME: "No, she doesn't even live in the city. She lives on her campus."

TEO: "What school?"

ME: "Why do you need to know all of that Tracy?"

TEO: "Let's not act like I can't find out for myself."

Punk ass bitch.

ME: "Whatever. Well find out from your police friends, cuz I'm not telling u. I don't see why u need to know all of that. Why we even talking about her in the first place?!"

TEO: "Because you haven't been honest with me Rodney! Why lie about having a girlfriend??"

ME: "She's not my girl tho! Like I said, she's who I've been rocking with since my last relationship ended!"

TEO: "Rodney I'm not stupid, I know what 'rocking with' means! Sashé is the bitch you play me to the left for, she's the one you're dicking down on the regular. Stop treating me like I'm a dumb bitch, u should know better at this point!"

ME: "That's what I'm saying, you think you know everything but u don't know shit. And you coming at me like you ain't in Ohio getting dick! You prolly fukcin' that nigga Larry - I ain't stupid either Tracy!"

TEO: "Larry and I are just friends. You can ask him yourself if you'd like."

ME: "Yeah whatever. You can ask HER for yourself then, if that's the case. I bet if I had police friends like you I'd find out the whole truth about that nigga. So whatever for real man."

TEO: "You don't even know what you're talking about Rodney. I don't have police friends. You don't have the slightest clue."

ME: "Yeah well I thought that's what this was about - you giving me a fukcin' clue! You done turned this bullshit around all on me! Wtf do u really want from me Tracy???"

TEO: "I just want u to be honest! Stop lying to me about this bitch. Stop taking advantage of me when u have her in your life to support you."

ME: "But it's not like that Tracy..."

TEO: "Then what's it like? You tell me about all this stress on your shoulders about Ronnie, and how u have no one in your corner like u need - yet u have HER. I never get to see u when I wanna see u because you live with this Sashé girl! You take my money, and u spend it on her."

ME: "Man u tripping Tracy. For real. We don't live together, and I'm not spending your money on her. Like for real, I don't even know where you're getting your info but the shit ain't all facts."

I was telling the truth here, as far as the intricate details went. Shay *wasn't* living with me yet; she was still down in the Burg in her last semester of school at the time. And she ain't have a clue I was even *talking* to Tracy...I had been going outta my way to hide all the extra money and gifts at home. What Tracy was alleging here was ridiculously off-base.

TEO: "So you're telling me that you don't live with this chick?"

ME: "I live alone Tracy, I can prove it."

TEO: "I want to believe u Rodney. I want to trust u and help u like I really want to. But I can't take the risk if you're just gonna be playing me. I can't defend this to my dad and convince him to stop digging. If you're just using me to get your rocks off I don't mind continuing to help with your sister, but if you're taken, you're taken. I'm not going to compete with a bitch that can't offer half of what I can."

I'm yawning again, ready to just fukcin' go to sleep.

ME: "I'm not fukcin' lying to you or using you! I told u I don't care about the shit u send me! If you wanna stop doing shit for me - fine! I'm not gonna keep telling u over and over that I don't live with this girl..."

TEO: "Ok Rodney."

Wait. Ok?

ME: "Ok? Ok what?"

TEO: "I'm going to believe u. I don't believe you're the person my dad thinks you are, and as much as you two are alike - I know you're not the selfish asshole that he can be. I'm not stupid, ok? I know u see females in Kansas City, I know you're doing your thing - I don't expect you to be 'faithful' or waiting on me. I'm just not going to be stupid enough to help you support some other bitch, especially with what I REALLY want to do for you."

ME: *"What are u talking about? Here you go with the indirect vague shit man. Like - what are u talking about?"*

TEO: *"Rodney just promise me you're not living with this bitch and that she's not who my dad thinks she is to you. If you're lying about this type of stuff; he can find out."*

ME: *"I mean wtf - who does he think she is to me? Whatever y'all think y'all know...I'm telling u - it ain't all facts."*

TEO: *"So then promise me. Promise me that you don't live together. And that she isn't your girlfriend from college."*

ME: *"Look, I promise those things aren't true. Now can we get past this shit with her?"*

TEO: *"Ok. If you make me regret this, I'm going to make u regret the day u ever thought you could play me for a fool. Don't make me have to go there Rodney, please."*

Her threats just come off as bullshit banter as I'm reading half-sleep. In fact, I dozed off for a second before I read her next message. It's the phone vibration that wakes me back up with a jerk. But it's what she *said* that left me stuck with intrigue for the rest of the morning:

TEO: "I have to put my phone on airplane mode, I'm taking off soon. So no need to reply. But listen up. I need u to delete all msgs between us from now on. If I text u from a different #, don't freak out. I have to start hiding you from him, and he's going to be monitoring my accounts. Don't worry ok? I have access to money he will never know about. He can't stop me from doing what I want to do like he thinks. If he could, he would have a long time ago. Just trust me on this, and don't lie to me about these chicks u deal with. That's all I ask. When I land I'll give u some more details on what I need from u. I'll talk to u soon."

*   *   *   *   *

<u>September 2007</u>
6:28pm

It was much too late to head to the barber shop now; I had long given that thought up. I shoulda *been* left the studio by now and working on my damage control at home with Sashé. Yet here I was, wrapping up this tale as Jaz played back my song one last time.

"The shit do sound good, nigga," Krush bobbed his head along with the music. "Real talk."

"Yeah, I know," I agreed. "You kilt that beat, bro."

"Right on."

"You coulda let me mix this shit by now," Jaz kept pleading his case. "This shit is done, bro."

Shaking my head to the beat, I replied, "Nah, man. I'm telling you – I gotta get a chick to ad-lib this muhfukca, bro; add some sound effects to it. Watch how I bring it to life."

"Shit...get the **Tracy** chick up in the studio, nigga!" Krush teased jokingly. "Tell her fly her ass on in this weekend, nigga."

"Nigga, you crazy!" I chuckled, biting my lip. "But for real – a nigga gotta start packing this weekend. I gotta be out the apartment at the end of the month. And shit – while we bullshitting...I ain't never even met that bitch in the flesh, nigga."

Jaz quickly butted in, "So, when y'all getting the keys to the new spot?"

Before I could answer, Krush hopped up and stood in between me and Jaz, close enough for me to smell the *Henny* on his breath, "Wait! What? What you mean? You never fukced this Tracy chick?"

"Bro, he still ain't never *met* that bitch, bro!" Jaz screamed.

"Man, *fukc* nah, nigga – you niggaz *lying* now, man!" Krush was livid and had heard just about enough. "You expect me to believe you got this chick you met *online*, sending you money – tryna fly you out on *trips* n'shit...but you never *met* her, bro? You telling me you ain't never took the bitch up on no offer to meet up? And she still kicking you down??"

"Shiiit," I raised my eyebrow arrogantly. "She kicking me down on a whole different level now though, nigga."

"I'm saying...*why* though?" Krush questioned the motives. "Why would you not meet up with the bitch? You said she wuttin' busted, nigga."

"Too risky, bro."

"So, is she cool with Shay now, nigga?" Krush kept probing like an eager kid in a classroom. "Y'all bout to move in together! I thought that was her deal-breaker, *right?*"

"Yeah, that's a good point, nigga!!! How you gon hide this move-in from her? You know she got eyes out here," Jaz shot me a look of real concern.

"*I got this,* bro. For real. Just trust a nigga on this. Tracy ain't as many steps ahead of me as she likes to think when it come to how I be moving."

"So, what about ya girl? The messages she seen?" Krush asked about the dilemma I still had to face. "I'm saying, nigga...I need to know how you handling this shit – on the real."

"Me, too, Rod. Sound like you got ya work cut out for you, for real. Shay ain't going for this shit, bro – especially now that y'all on the *ménage* shit with ole girl."

Jaz was right...I had my *work* cut out for me. And it wuttin' until he put it like *that* that I actually had an idea about how to balance all of this shit out before it got completely out of hand. Suddenly...I had a plan on how to deal with Shay. It was a longshot, but it just might work.

"Yo!!! Bro, is that shit finished burning to disc?? I

gotta get outta here, yo. I don't know why I didn't think of this shit before!"

"What, nigga?" Jaz spun around in his chair. "What you thinking?"

I started grabbing my things, moving quickly before either of them tried to stop me. I knew I ain't have much time; I needed to catch Tracy before she went to her next meeting. Once she gets in these damn meetings, she takes forever to text back.

"Bro, I gotta go! I'ma come back for the disc – lemme go handle this shit, though, my nigga!! I'll get up!" I threw my duffle bag over my shoulder.

Within 20 seconds I was out of the front door of **64111 Studio** and in my *Dodge Intrepid*, **Keisha** – speeding down *Summit Street*. Once I got to the bottom of the hill, I stopped and pulled over – so I could text in peace. I needed to be alone, so I could be focused.

*   *   *   *   *

<u>7:09pm</u>

When I finally got to my apartment door and started to unlock it, **Shay** opened it up, anxiously awaiting my arrival. She had this look of *conflict* on her face, one that I rarely ever seen. I mean, to this day, we still haven't had a real fight. The chemistry between us was on a different plateau and I'd spent a lot of time and energy to try not to fukc that up.

"Hey, babe," I greeted her softly, testing the waters.

"Hello, *Mr. Henderson,*" Shay replied mockingly.

222

"Don't start...please. It's been a long day."

She immediately helped my duffle bag off my shoulder and took my hand, guiding me to the couch as we stepped over a couple of packing boxes. Before we sat down, she adjusted the burgundy cover...which was damn near off the couch completely again, exposing the dingy furniture.

"I'm sure it has," she switched to a more concerned voice tone. "Well, come on; sit down. You know we need to talk."

"Ok. So let's."

She reaches down to the floor, picking up my *work phone,* and sits it on the table in front of us. Before she speaks, she then puts her legs across my lap and sits back on the arm rest, getting comfortable, "I'm listening."

"Ok, so," I started carefully. "It's not what you think, though!"

"Ok, well then you tell me what it is. You know how this works, Mister. *No secrets.* If it's not what I'm thinking, then what is it?"

I sat up straight and took a deep breath. Shay reached behind me to adjust the couch covers once again as they slumped down with my weight. "Babe, I am really tired of these dang covers, seriously," she sighed.

"Trust me, I know."

"Ok, so no more stalling," Shay folded her arms. "Come on. I'm listening."

"Damn, I wuttin' even stalling – you made the comment about the *couch covers!*

"Baaabe," she whined impatiently. "Tell me about this list of addresses."

"Ok," I took a deep breath. "So…you know she's into real estate. She sent me a list of addresses that she researched and wants me to go look at them for her."

Sashé paused momentarily, taking it in, "Hmm. Ok. She wants to buy more property here now? I mean, I thought you said her dad was watching closely? I don't get why she would want to have legitimate business in her name that can be traced back to her. Like…that's never made sense to me!!!"

"I mean…I guess this is part of that other shit she's into, babe. I don't know."

"Oh, right! Because she's just soooo sure her police dad can't find out she's into illegal shit!?"

"Shay, boo. Relax," I stopped her. "Don't say it like that. She's had him under control for a long time now. Just go with it. I got this, for real."

Shay was noticeably frustrated and cried out, "I'm just saying, babe! Do you know how hard it is for me to believe half the stuff you tell me about this *Tracy* girl? Kris tells me it all sounds made up, Daddy!"

"I get it, but you know how this works around here, babe. Kris doesn't," I rubbed her shoulder and gave her forehead a light peck. "I'm telling you what I know about the situation, when I know about it. For now, Tracy just got me looking at these properties – sending her pictures n'shit. That's what the list was about. When she gives me further instruction, I'll worry about what's next."

"So, other than the properties thingy – you haven't been talking to her lately about other stuff? Has she sent you anything recently that I don't know about?"

"I mean, it's just been the properties thing lately. That's really all she been talking about."

"Babe, don't hold out on me," Shay warned me to tread cautiously. "Do you even *remember* what you didn't erase out of your work phone??? Do we need to look through it together? It's right here."

I glanced at the phone on the table, shaking my head. It was hard to get shit past Shay at this point; she was a student of **The Art** by way of me. And when she made that last comment...I knew I had to stick to my formula of *giving up a little to get away with a lot.*

The truth is, Sashé had known about my dealings with Tracy *as soon as* Tracy mentioned her name to me. With everything going on with my sister being on the run and how close Shay and I were becoming, I wuttin' gon' let this Ohio chick threaten what I had worked so hard to achieve. So, after we had dinner the weekend the Vegas trip didn't happen, I came clean to Sashé about what had been going on. Well...*almost* clean anyway.

"Babe, it's no need for that. I'm not hiding anything, I know what you saw. And other than money she's sent me for Ronnie's books...she ain't sent nothing else."

"Are you lying to me?"

I was. Tracy sends me money *all the time.* In fact, at this point, there's times when she sends money for me to *drop off* to people – for Tracy's *other* business. Shay only knew what she *needed* to know. And for the purposes of protecting her in case shit ever hit the fan...I never told Shay *half* the truth about the *illegal* shit Tracy was into.

However, she at least knew, like I now knew, that

Tracy was *not* the square, legitimate girl that she appeared to be. She was the daughter of a former street hustler who decided to go straight and narrow after meeting his first love, Tracy's late mother. Her father, **Mr. Thomas Evanston,** had been part of a drug network that moved heroin through several states in the early 80's and he tried with all his power to bury and hide this dark past from his only child.

But, as with anybody who tries to run from their origins, there were still people lingering around that never forgot. Mr. Evanston's older brother and Tracy's uncle, **Terrell**, was his main partner while he was in the streets. When *Tommy E* chose to go work on the *opposite* side of the law, he and his brother never spoke a word to each other again – despite the fact that Tracy's mom continued to have a healthy family relationship with Terrell and his kids.

As a result, Tracy was groomed and schooled to the game at an early age, taught by one of the best how to hide it from those who mattered. Along with her first cousin, **Tristan**, they were still heavily involved in all the street shit you could think of, right under her Daddy's nose.

But as far as *Shay* knew – Tracy was only involved in some *petty credit card fraud* I was helping her out with. Shay knew nothing about *Tristian* or *the drugs* and I had no plans on ever bringing her fully up to speed. Once I came clean about this gift-happy Tracy chick I had met online...I had to pick and choose what truths to tell Shay for her own good. This was some pretty deep shit, even for me to be dealing with.

"I'm not lying, Shay."

She stared me dead in the eye and initially didn't budge or make a sound. After a few seconds, she finally declared, "Well, I don't believe you. You should have told me about the properties stuff before I went through your phone to find out."

"Babe, don't do that. Come on. You know I'm not hiding shit."

"Well, I still think you need to make it up to me!!! You weren't being upfront with it either! We had a *deal*. And I could tell from the messages that she still wants to *meet up* with you, so I don't know how much longer I'll even be cool with you still talking to her. Seriously."

I was afraid of this. But also *expecting* it, which is why I immediately texted Tracy when I left the studio. I knew that moving in to this new place soon with Shay was gon' throw another yet wrench in this setup I had with Miss Buckeye. And even though I'm walking a real thin line at this point…I just can't give up what Tracy does for me. Not now. The shit is too major.

About six months ago, Tracy explained to me that her and Tristian were looking to expand their business to my home state. I'll admit that I was beyond hesitant to get involved at first, with everything going on with Ronnie and her case. But after hearing the cousins out, the opportunity was just too good to pass up.

Tristian had followed in his father's footsteps and became a major factor in the *ecstasy pill* game. He had a connect in Kansas he could buy wholesale from, so when Tracy found out I was really living in Kansas just across state lines instead of at my aunt's on the Missouri side — she suggested they start using me as a courier to facilitate the transactions more discreetly.

My job was simple. Tracy had purchased several foreclosed homes in Missouri that her real estate shell company planned to renovate. They would hire a legit construction crew and contractors to work fulltime on the properties before putting the houses back on the market after a few months. But before the renovations were finished, Tracy would text me an address that Trist would be shipping a package to.

My job was to visit the property on the day of delivery, posing as the point of contact for the real estate group. They even sent me a *I. Evanston & Associates, LLP* shirt with my name on it to make it look real. The random packages would contain supplies or parts for the home…but hidden somewhere, there was always an envelope filled with cash. After intercepting the re-up money, I would then make *two* stops – one trip to meet with **Skip**, Tristian's wholesale pill connect, and then one trip to link up with **BoBo**, the guy moving the pills in Missouri for Tracy and Trist.

Skip would travel from his residence in *Topeka, KS* to bring me the pills. We would then meet at random spots with a public restroom, but the transaction would always be the same routine. No words, no interactions. I would arrive early, head to a stall with a black duffle bag filled with bootleg CD's covering up the money envelope, and pretend to be taking a dump. Skip would park his car at a gas pump and come in the restroom with the same type of duffle bag – *his* filled with the pill re-up. After making sure no one else was in there with us, we would then swap bags by him doing the switcharoo under the stall and we'd go on about our business.

I would then take the bag of pills across state lines to Missouri to meet up with *BoBo* in the city, who in turn distributed the product to his dealers across my home state. BoBo never exchanged any money with me and I had no idea about how he would pay Trist and Tracy back for fronting the work. All I knew was that he was their new Missouri distributor and had been personally recommended by their plug, *Skip*. It was never my business to know what happened after I done my part and I never cared to know.

After BoBo had the pills in hand, I would text Tracy and she would send me a *Money Gram* payment the next day. The amounts varied and would sometimes include extra to pay Ronnie's lawyer or put money on her commissary. The system worked and, like Tracy told me, essentially changed my life in general. Though I couldn't let anyone close to me know what I had signed up for, the extra bread started opening up new doors for us all.

Then, after a few months, Tracy and Trist decided we needed to switch things up to further increase their profit margin by even more. They shared with me a new plan to relocate Skip away from his Topeka, KS home to a spot closer to me – in hopes of saving money and time on his travel routine. Up until then, Skip was driving about an hour from Topeka to Overland Park or Olathe, KS to meet me for the exchanges. Tracy thought it made sense to look into some properties in my local area that didn't need renovation for Skip to move to. And so, she told me she'd be sending a list of potential homes for me to go peep out before they made the purchase and proposed paying me an additional 20% for my troubles.

Of course, with how deeply I was involved now, this changeup wouldn't be an issue for me. I had learned how to hide most of the extra cash flow from Shay and figured out how to keep Tracy at bay from constantly questioning me about my girl at home. Again…I knew I was walking a helluva thin line with all the shit that I was juggling. If we could just see this Skip relocation through, the additional money I knew I had coming was my biggest motivator to keep everything intact.

But at the same time…I still gotta take care of *home*. Keeping Shay happy at all costs was still my main priority. I knew she read those messages from Tracy and even though Shay knew most of the truth, I also knew she'd be upset and would need extra reassurance to go with my explanation. So, I seen this tantrum coming and made a quick play before coming home to face Sashé.

See, Tracy knew better than to text my **work phone** unless it was quick transaction related. And since she had come clean about her dad and how discreet we needed to move going forward, the both of us had become real consistent in how we communicated. Her texting my work phone was out of sync, *especially* not knowing who might see the messages. It was sloppy. She knew better. And it was something I knew I could hold her accountable for.

Tracy was well aware that I was moving to a new place of my own soon. I anticipated that she'd be all on top of trying to figure out if I was moving in with another bitch, so I had the lease paperwork set up to where Shay's name wuttin' listed as a renter. My bases were covered there. But knowing Tracy...I still needed to put *her* focus and energy elsewhere for a little while.

So, before I drove home to face the music with Shay, I snapped on Tracy about texting the work phone – made it out like *my boss* seen it and I gave her a big guilt trip for the ages. By the time I was done, my newfound Ohio connect was in full-blown *apology mode* and willing to make it up to me however I asked.

"Babe, stop it. You know we gotta keep her around a little longer. Stop fussing; quit acting like that. Let me just make it up to you, like I said."

"How? How do you think you're gonna do that?" Shay smacked her lips.

"Well, for starters…when we move, these raggedy ass couches ain't coming with us. We need to go look at new furniture tomorrow," I smiled, full of pride and confidence.

"Wait, what? We're getting new couches?" Shay propped up on the pillows, twirling her toes. "Shut up! How?"

"She sending a *Money Gram* tonight for me to get a new set. You wanna ride with me to go get it?"

Sashé was beaming with glee and excitement, "Are you lying to me? Daddy, no you *didn't!!!* Are you serious? Ok…how much…how much??? She's not gonna find out we're moving in together – right? Oh my God, Daddy!!!"

"Don't worry about all'at," I reassured her. "Just trust me like you been doing – alright? Stick to the plan like we talked about, no matter what. I got this."

Shay just looked at me and shook her head in reluctant disbelief…but after all of the shit we'd been through leading up to this point, she knew she was my real and *official* partner-in-crime. She didn't quite understand how or why somebody like Tracy could feel the need to take care of me from so many miles away. I knew it had a lot to do with the infamous **Son's Curse,** but neither one of us really needed to understand the *'why'* completely. She'd felt that same need in her own way when *we* first crossed each other's paths, so Shay recognized there was something about me that had this mysterious effect on women. And I knew, *whatever* it was, as long as my girl could benefit from it *with me*, I had everything under control.

"Ok, Daddy," she lowered her eyes at me, in the pure admiration I was accustomed to. "I trust you."

"Good girl," I bit my lip. "She should be sending the money in about an hour if you wanna come with."

Shay's eyes lit up again with excitement, "You know I do, Daddy! Let me just hop in the shower first – I won't take long, I promise."

"Take your time, girl," I reached for my duffle bag on the floor, looking for my phone. "I think she just now getting out her meeting."

Sashé scurried off to the bedroom to get her overnight bag, "Ok, ok – well lemme hurry up before Kris gets here, babe!"

I paused from scrolling through my phone to look up, realizing what she just said, "Kris? She on her way here, now, babe?"

"Yes!" Shay yelled from the bathroom as she turned the shower on. "I didn't know how our conversation would go and I asked her to come get me – just in case!"

"Damn, that's fukced up," I shook my head, smiling. "So, y'all was gon' break up with me?!?!"

"Oh, Daddy…stop acting like that! I just didn't know what was *happening!* Gimme a break!"

"Mmm hmm, whatever!" I yelled over the water. "Y'all ain't leaving me…shut that shit up!"

"Can she come with us, too, Daddy??? And can we get ice cream?!?!"

I checked my **Inbox** for any new replies from Tracy, but her last message was almost 45 minutes ago. "Of course, babe. Whatever you want – you know that."

Ever since this summer when we finally had our first successful *ménage* with Kris, the curvy Russian had become our recurring play toy on most nights. I fukcin' loved having her around, especially because she always made Shay's mood better. Not that Shay's mood was ever shitty like that – but whenever Kris was around, the positive vibes were just on a thousand. They were comfortable with each other and their chemistry was unmatched. To cheat on this situation would be asinine on my behalf, right?

Kris only knew the bare minimum about my dealings with Tracy, but she at least knew enough to know the situation *existed*. And I wuttin' bothered at all by Shay calling her bff for a potential rescue mission had things gone left with our discussion. It made sense, actually.

What a long fukcin' day, bruh…

Nigga, who you telling?

Yo ass almost got us caught up, nigga!

Man, get the fukc outta here, nigga! I'm the glue holding all dis shit together!!! Don't front…

Yeah, whatever nigga. I'm sick of yo shit!

Nigga, spark that blunt up and quit bullshitting! Hoe ass nigga!

Now that I finally had a moment to myself, I took a deep breath and started getting settled – pulling my gray hoodie over my head and stripping down to a wife-beater and sweats. The *Henny* and bud rounds from the studio hadn't quite worn off yet, but that ain't stop me from pouring another drink in the kitchen and heading to my computer desk to light the blunt waiting for me in the ashtray. Turning some slow jams on, I realized the **beast** had the right idea. It really *had* been a long ass day — straight up.

Before it slipped my mind, I grabbed my cell phone and shot Jaz a text to let him know the coast was clear:

ME: "We all good in the hood! Cyber pimp mode ACTIVATED lololol"

JAZ: "My dawg!!!! Call me in the morning nigga!!!"

After about five more minutes, Kris arrived at the front door and knocked lightly. Her knocks were so gentle that I doubt if Shay even heard 'em over the music and loud running water. When I opened the door, Kris looked surprised to see me.

"Hello, Kristina," I stepped to the side to welcome her in, grinning with mischief and reaching to help with her bags.

"Oh, hi," she giggled as she pinched my cheek. "I didn't think you'd be home already, Mr. Playboy."

"Well, I'm happy to see you, too, boo," I teased as she floated past me in her pink stilettos. "I can't get my hug, though?"

Kris paused momentarily to scan the living room and kitchen, "Where is Shay?"

"She in the shower – she'll be out soon. She told me you was 'bout to pull up…errthang straight now, though."

She smirked at me, "Mmm hmm…it better be, sir!"

"Can I get my hug???" I repeated myself, this time more sternly.

"Yes, Daddy," Kris giggled again, smacking her lips like a brat. "You so silly, boy."

Dropping the *Gucci* bags to the floor, I took a step in her direction, looking her up and down with lustful intent. Kris was probably the baddest white girl I had ever been around at the time, and tonight was no exception. Nights like these, her sex appeal was nearly effortless – as she stood there in her red stretch pants and halter top, taking her jean jacket off. After the day I'd had, my hormones were on edge. Kris caught me looking at her meaty pussy print and bit her lip as she wrapped her arms around my neck to give me a warm and welcome embrace.

"Oh, so I'm *Daddy'* now?" I lowered my voice, pulling her in closer with my lips at her forehead. Her vanilla mist scent mixed in with her tanned skin contrasted against my darkness instantly gave me a rush.

"When you not acting bad," she looked up at me, her soft lips grazing mine.

"I thought you liked when I'm bad," I licked my chops, returning her graze with my moist tongue.

She began tracing my left ear with her fingernails, instantly turned on just that quick, "Hmmm….I do. But that's differe…"

I cut her words short as I grabbed her round ass cheek with one hand and a lock of her dirty blonde hair with the other, jerking her head back so I could see her quivering neck in plain view. Startled, she let out a soft moan as I kissed her collar bone, breathing her in.

Instinctively, her fingernail traces then turned into anxious, aggressive digging in my upper back. She melted in my arms and curled her left leg around me, causing my **wooD** to instantly wake up. We bumped into the table in front of the couch, regaining balance by pulling each other in even closer.

We stood still for a second, eye-fukcing each other. I could smell the *Moscato* on her breath and I was sure she could smell the *Hennessy* and GG on mine. Her nipples started poking out of her skimpy top as she grinded into my manhood, causing me to thrust into her warm crotch. I could tell she was horny and wanted me and suddenly my adrenaline was guiding the **beast**. I grabbed her firmly by her exposed waist, kissing and drooling on her busty cleavage.

"You…better…stop before you…hmmm…get something…started," Kris whispered in between heavy pants. Naturally, she briefly glanced over at the steam from Shay's shower blowing out of the cracked bathroom door behind me to my right.

I ignored her warning and instead paid more attention to her *body language*, biting her left nipple through her shirt. She quickly pushed up on me…and I couldn't tell if she was trying to nudge me away or what. At this point I didn't care. I willingly allowed her body weight to fall on me as we slowly stumbled backwards onto the couch together. My hands then moved to her stretch pants, tugging them down in sync with Kris collapsing in my lap. She started twisting and squirming, helping me get them down to her knees before she stood up and dropped them to her ankles. As expected, she wasn't wearing any panties. Kris hardly ever wore panties.

"Damn, girl," I mumbled under my breath, licking my lips as her blonde landing strip stared me in the face.

She put her hands on her hips and stood on display for me, her engorged clit peeking through her fat lips. "Oops," she said with a devilish grin.

Without another moment's hesitation and with no regard for her best friend in the other room, I lunged forward and pulled Kris towards me by her thick thighs. As my nose made contact with her smooth pelvis, she grabbed the top of my head to brace herself. Her pussy lips were already drenched, as if she had been playing with herself in the car.

"Look who's acting bad now, though," I kissed her left leg, peeling her sticky wet clit hood back. "You missed me, lil baby?"

"You so bad, Rodney."

"Nah, that's *you*, girl," I ran my tongue across her slit, making her tremble and grip my head tighter. "You a bad influence."

She propped her left leg up on my shoulder as I started devouring her flower, slurping softly. She tasted so fresh and gushy, I couldn't help but moan in satisfaction. Kris then followed suit and let out a long sigh of lustful relief, "Oh my gaaawd…fuck."

I reached under her legs, spreading them slightly so I could palm both ass cheeks. Squeezing firmly, I then forced her whole pussy in my eager mouth, slurping greedily and sloppily in between tongue flickers. Her heavy breathing quickened, right on schedule.

By now, I knew Kris's body almost as well as Shay's. I knew what drove her crazy and I knew how to make her cum repeatedly. Kris liked her pussy eaten nearly identical to the way Shay preferred – light licks and sensual sucking. The major difference between Kris and Shay was that Kris actually liked to be *fingered* more. But in this moment, I decided to tease her. Knowing she was craving two or three fingers inside while I slurped away…I kept my hands planted securely on her ass, going to work solely with my mouth.

I could still hear the water running in the bathroom with Shay splashing away in the shower. Luckily, the loud stream was helping the music drown out the sound of Kris's high-pitched, intense moans. Shay wuttin' the jealous type…but the way I was covering my chin in her best friend's juices might raise an eyebrow.

I didn't care, though. Kris kept squirming and jerking on my face and my dick was rock fukcin' hard in my joggers. I was turned on to the max.

"Mmm hmm," I smacked my lips, looking up at her with her head leaning back. I noticed that she had somehow came outta her halter top and was now ass-naked in my living room, her perky tits sitting perfect above my dome.

I leaned forward, nearly hanging off the couch now. Her pussy was throbbing, clenching up as I stuck my whole tongue in. I knew she was getting close…and I smirked as I suddenly pulled away.

"Fuck, Rodneeey," she whined, looking down at me in agony. "I was 'bout to cum."

I stood up, swiftly pulling my joggers and boxer briefs down. My dick popped out, slapping against her right leg as she stepped back to give me some space. Then I grabbed her by the neck and looked her deep in the eye as I whispered with pure dominance, "You not 'bout to cum 'til I fukcin' *tell* you you can cum. Now grab my dick."

"Yes, Daddy," she gasped as she complied without hesitation. "Yes, sir."

Her organic submission took me over the edge and I felt that familiar energy come over me. The first time this happened years ago, I must've blacked out. It's a new day now, though; I've been here before.

"Take them fukcin' pants off and bend dat ass over," I commanded, nudging her to my right so we could switch places as I moved the living room table out the way.

Kris swiftly kicked her stretch pants to the side and bent over on the couch arm, pulling the burgundy cover out of place again. Moaning with anticipation, she then reached under her legs and started playing with her pussy, rubbing desperately. I jacked my **wooD** off for a few seconds, salivating at her pink asshole. The arch in her back was immaculate as always.

"Spread them ass cheeks apart, girl," I continued spewing demands, breathing hard. "And don't fukcin' move. Be the fukc still."

"Ok, Daddy…but be gentle, please?" she whined, looking back at the rage in my eyes. She had this look as if she knew I would have no regard for her request.

And she was absolutely right…

I entered her slowly…pausing once I got halfway in, allowing her to relax her muscles on my thickness. She bit her lip and her eyes rolled back as she laid her head on the armrest.

"Fuuuuck…oh my God," she whimpered, tensing up.

"Breathe," I told her. "Relax, lil baby. You got it…"

She stood on her tippy-toes and eased back on my dick…cautiously taking it balls deep. I grabbed her waist and pulled back, holding her in place. Her pussy was so gotdamn tight and warm. I could feel myself throbbing against her walls as they clamped down on my shaft repeatedly. I grunted, drooling on her lower back tattoo.

"There you go," I encouraged her. "Good girl."

She moaned in bliss, as if those words suddenly motivated her. Within a split second she starting throwing it back at a steady pace, slamming against my pulsating meat. After a few strokes, I could see her cream painting me up and I bit my lip.

"Didn't I tell yo ass to be still?" I thrusted deep and slapped her left cheek with my right hand, causing her to yelp. "And did you cum on my dick without me telling you to???"

"Hmmm…yes, Daddy. I'm sorry, Daddy," she panted. "I…fuck…I can't…I can't help it, Daddy…"

"Shut the fuck up, girl," I growled at her. *You think I'm playing wit yo ass!*

"No, baby…hmm…I'm…nah…I'm nottt. Ouuuch!! Rodneeey! Go slooow," she winced in pleasurable pain as I dug deeper.

"What the fukc you just call me, girl?"

Kris squirmed and tried to scoot forward but I pulled her back towards me and thrusted with more intensity. Her pussy clamped down, trying to force me out. But I wuttin' having it. I bent down slightly to force my dick upward, hitting her g-spot.

"I'm sorry…hmmm…I'm sorry, Daddy! I did…I didn't mean it…"

"Yes the fukc you did, bitch! Cum'ere – gimme this shit, girl!!!"

I lost all consideration and started pounding away, banging her limp body against the couch as it banged against the wall below the kitchen bar counter. Her moans and yelps intensified and I could hear her juicy pussy splashing with each stroke. It was at that point that I noticed the water in the bathroom had gone silent. Shay was apparently done with her shower…and now I was all but positive she could hear what was transpiring in the living room.

I leaned forward and wrapped my left arm around Kris's neck, covering her mouth up. She started licking and biting the palm of my hand as she took my **wooD**, breathing heavily and trying to brace herself. I had her right where I wanted her now.

"Oh my God, yessss! Hmmm…fukc me, Daddy! Ohhhh fuuuukc…it's so…hmmm…hard!" Kris started moaning loudly, as if she *wanted* Shay to hear us from the bathroom.

Suddenly just as inspired, I started rubbing her pink asshole while I groaned in a **beastly** rage. Sweat drenched my forehead and dripped down to her neck. "I want chu to cum again for me, Krissy baby. Cum all over Daddy's dick…"

We were in total sync now, our bodies rocking back and forth with primal lust. My thumb slipped inside her moist ass and her pussy started gripping me repeatedly. I felt her teeth sink into my wrist as she bit down hard, struggling to take my aggressive strokes.

I heard Shay walking around in the bedroom but I gave no fukcs in this moment. Sashé understood me. She understood that few of her friends could resist my energy. She knew I liked being sneaky…but she also knew that the constant urge I had to sneak around was no longer my biggest obstacle.

Her footsteps were light against the carpet as she finally approached me and Kris. She had only dried off halfway, and her huge tits were still damp. I glanced to my right and licked my lips as Shay's eyes locked on her bff bent over, taking my thick endowment. Without saying a word, she took her hand to my forehead to smear sweat all over her palm. Kneeling on the couch beside Kris, she then slowly started licking her fingers, tasting it. This drove both me and Kris nuts.

"Hmmm…you so fukcin' nasty," I whispered, breathing heavily and leaning back to take in the scene. "You like watching me fukc your friend, baby?"

"Mmm hmm…you know I do, Daddy," she licked her lips, drool running down her chin.

Kris stuck her tongue out to catch Shay's mouth juice and the duo began kissing passionately. Their two naked bodies in front of me looked like heaven. And Kris's pussy hugging my **wooD** so tightly had me in pure bliss. I reached out to nudge Shay, prompting her to bend over next to her friend.

"Lemme see dat fat ass pussy from the back, Shay baby," I commanded. "Keep your tongue in her mouth. Yeah…just like dat…"

Sashé complied without resistance and quickly turned around to arch her ass in the air for me. She then rested her head against the couch and grabbed both of her ankles, continuing her drool-swapping with Kris while I humped like a madman…

This raunchy ebony & ivory combo never got old to me. I'd prolly fukced the two of them together over a hunnid times since this past summer. But each and every time, it was passionate and full of excitement. The effect it started to take on my already overgrown ego was beyond evident, though.

I had two bad stripper bitchez at the crib who kept me fukced, fed, and focused…while also fattening my pockets. On top of that – I had *another* bitch miles away in Ohio, who I had never *met* physically, *also* keeping my pockets full.

This was the type of lifestyle most niggaz could only dream about, yet it had fallen in my lap without being forced. The **cyber pimpin'** aspect was all new territory for me, no doubt, but at the same time, it felt like I *belonged* here. With Shay being my partner-in-crime, it felt like *we* belonged here. It didn't matter that I was the only one in the world who knew the *full* truth about the tangled web I was weaving.

This is **The Art of Cheating** – the only thing that matters is never getting caught. As long as I covered my ass and kept playing my cards right, *karma* would never stand a chance…

I got this.

Yeah, nigga. For NOW, at least...

FIN.
(Until We Cheat Again)

ABOUT THE AUTHOR

"HoLLyRod" – the author and creator of the highly controversial and raunchy storyline, *The Art of Cheating* – is the alter-ego and pseudonym for established writer Rodney L. Henderson Jr.

Since graduating with a Business Administration degree in Computer Information Systems from the *University of Central Missouri*, Henderson has showcased his writing skills in various forms of art – including radio commercials and music, as well as poetry and promo spots for fashion companies such as *DymeWear Inc* and *Ridikulus Kouture LLC.*

HoLLyRod's short story mini-series titled **The Art of Cheating Episodes** introduces readers to the many characters and mystery behind **HoLLyWorld** and *The Art of Cheating,* while chronicling the ups and downs of infidelity through experiences based on real life. The ongoing series has been re-released in a special Extended Author's Cut Edition.

**AVAILABLE IN eBOOK and PAPERBACK FORMATS!!!
AUDIO BOOKS COMING SOON!!!**

Henderson currently resides in his home state of Missouri and spends most of his time managing and writing for *Angela Marie Publishing, LLC* – a company named after his late mother.

The Art of Cheating Episodes is published under *Lurodica Stories,* an erotica division of the publishing company.

"I just want to continue to be inspired at the notion of making her proud and keep my promise to share my talents with the world."

www.HoLLyRods.com
www.facebook.com/TheArtOfCheating
www.twitter.com/TheCheatGods

<u>Also by HoLLyRod</u>

The Art of Cheating Episodes
(Extended Author's Cut Edition)

SEASON 1
Episode 1 - Sassy
Episode 2 – Hangover
Episode 3 - HoLLy BeLLigerence
Episode 4 - KeLLy's Revenge
Episode 5 - The HooKup
Episode 6 – Ménages

SEASON 2
Episode 1 - Cyber Pimpin'
Episode 2 - Campus Record
Episode 3 – A Date with Karma
Episode 4 – The Wedding Party
Episode 5 – HoLLy & Sug

SEASON 3
(Coming Soon)